Reviving Love

A Black Hollow Story

Cassidy K. O'Connor

Dedication

I would like to thank Shawn Mendes, his latest song *In My Blood* was an inspiration to me while creating Adam's character. I felt the pain in his song and knew it's exactly how Adam would have felt.

One

"It's been two years Sarah, they locked Hank up and threw away the key. Asald and I love you and we want to see you happy. Even Alex is starting to question your lackluster love life."

Sarah scowled at her friend Penny, how dare she insinuate her little boy was thinking about her dating life.

"All we're saying is you could use a weekend of adult time. My parents are going to keep Christian for us and they've offered to keep Alex too. Come with us to Black Hollow, Asald promises his friends are awesome and we're going to have a lot of fun."

Sarah's nails tapping in rhythm on the table seemed way more interesting than making eye contact with her best friend. She knew she was right, she had lived like a nun for so long now she didn't know how to break out of the prison she had built around herself.

"You trust Asald and me, believe me when I say Alex will be safe and you will have fun. Besides you know you're as curious as I am to meet his friends. We've talked to them so many times on the phone, they'll be offended if you snub them and don't come."

"Well, that's not fair, playing the guilt card on me." Sarah sighed as Penny wiggled her eyebrows, smiling like a loon. "Fine, if I agree to go with you this weekend can we agree that I don't have to be forced into another dating situation for at least six months?"

"Six months! That's crazy." Penny exclaimed as Sarah quirked her eyebrow and leveled a hard stare that froze Penny in her place, before finally relenting. "Fine, six months free from our intervention into your sex life."

Satisfied with her agreement she gave in. "So, tell me about this grand weekend you have planned? What do I need to pack? Where do I call for a hotel room? And where the hell is Black Hollow, Massachusetts, I've never heard of it."

"I haven't been there before either but I can't wait to go. It's a small coastal town just North of Salem. From what he's told me they are even more eccentric than Salem and celebrate all kinds of paranormals not just witches. They throw this huge Halloween party every year that is by invitation only." Sarah grabbed a towel and started drying the dishes Penny was washing. "We are staying at an Inn and I already booked you a room next to ours."

"Someone was confident I was going to cave."

"More like determined to hound you till you let me have my way. We're also picking up costumes in town so don't worry about packing anything special. All you have to do is meet me at my parents Thursday after work and we'll drive up."

Childish laughter filled the room as Asald came into the kitchen with their son Christian on his shoulders and Alex wrapped around his leg being dragged.

"Good news babe, she's going with us this weekend." Asald's look of surprise meant he hadn't expected his wife to be successful either.

Asald pulled his leg forward so he could see Alex's face. "I guess that means you are playing big brother to Christian this weekend. Grandma and Grandpa have lots of fun things planned and really want to you stay with them. What do you think?"

Alex popped up off the ground and melted his mother's heart with a huge smile. Two years ago they'd been living in a shelter, abused and alone. Now they had Asald and Penny and their entire family had adopted them. She would be forever grateful to Penny's parents for treating him like any of their other grandchildren. Tears burned her eyes; she swallowed hard around the lump in her throat.

"Can I stay with them, mom?"

"Of course, you can. Now grab your backpack and let's get home."

"Bye Birdman!"

Sarah shook her head at Alex's nickname for Asald and hugged everyone goodbye.

***

As soon as the front door closed Asald gave Penny a look of concern. "Are you really sure you want to do this? Are you ready for her to know all about me and my world?"

"For two years Alex has sworn you can fly and saved him on that roof. She has never believed him before so I don't think she will suddenly figure things out after one party. However, I hate keeping this one huge part of our life a secret from her so I'm hoping to break it to her this weekend."

"I trust you so if you are ready for her to know the real me than so am I. Now, let's get Christian in bed and go work on making him a little sister or brother."

Two

Sarah stood staring at her closet, it was hard to pack for the unexpected. At least she was used to Fall in New England so it wasn't tough to throw in enough layers to make an outfit for any situation. Hoping she had grabbed enough choices she left to meet up with Penny at her parents' house to drop the kids off. This was the first time she would be sleeping away from Alex and the idea paralyzed her. She was relieved that he was excited to be going, this meant his father hadn't completely destroyed him.

"I'm really doing this aren't I?" Penny rolled her eyes at Sarah's mumbled and repeated question.

"Would you like some liquid courage to help calm you down? We can fill a thermos before we go?"

"No it's fine, I'll be fine, let's just get on the road so I can't back out." Sarah saw the compassion on her friend's face, Penny had seen Sarah at her worst, her most broken and understood how big of a step this was for her.

They pulled into Penny's driveway as Asald was putting the last of their bags in the trunk. After a quick kiss for Penny, he grabbed her bags and moved them to his car. "Okay ladies, let's do this."

He practically ran around the car to get going, he was meeting these friends for the first time as well. From what Penny told her, Asald had been doing some kind of genealogy research and found a group of people who were similar to him. She assumed that meant maybe their ancestors were from the same area or something? She wasn't really sure when she pushed them for details they mumbled a bit then moved on. Was there a skeleton in his family tree he didn't want to talk about? Either way, she was glad he was making new friends, like her, he was an orphan and had no family so she hoped these people would change all of that for him.

She watched out the window as the miles went by, her mind wandered until she jerked awake realizing she had fallen asleep.

"Welcome back sleepy head, you were out for a while. We just got off the interstate, it won't be too much longer now."

After a few turns, she noticed the beautiful oranges, reds, and yellows of the leaves had faded and everything was either brown or barren. It was actually breathtakingly beautiful seeing the naked branches reaching across the road towards each other almost like lovers reuniting. The buildings they passed weren't shiny or new and the town all but took her breath away. She knew they catered to tourists by playing up the paranormal but this was amazing.

The apothecary had signs in the window exclaiming a sale on love potions. The blood bank had fangs with dripping blood in their logo.

Competing bars on the corner had signs listing who wasn't allowed in their establishments. Stoney's on the left didn't allow witches, fairies, or any other creature that were not part animal. Thirst had one very clear rule: no animal shifters of any kind could enter.

At the stop sign, she heard Penny gasp as a group of children crossed the street all holding brooms and each had an animal with them. One of the kids black cat was jumping towards another girl who had a Raven perched on her shoulder. The boy at the end was barely swinging his cauldron, probably because the largest toad in history was peeking outside of it.

"When I fell asleep did we cross into another dimension? This is incredible. I've visited Salem, they have nothing on this town." She couldn't help the double take when she saw a perfectly normal looking girl serving coffee outside of 'Hells Brew'. She didn't seem fazed at all standing in front of two large men with black wings lightly fluttering while they sipped their coffee.

"The guys said the town goes all out for the month of October. Everyone gets involved and plays up their characters, I guess they weren't kidding." Asald gave Penny a nervous glance. She thought it was cute, he seemed hesitant to meet his friends.

They turned off the main road and followed a street around to a surprisingly quaint looking Inn that didn't seem to fit in with the rest of the town's aesthetic.

"The Daydreamer Inn, this looks pleasant." Penny's reassuring smiles gave away how nervous she was about their accommodations being a rundown looking motel.

Penny and Sarah each grabbed a bag while Asald grabbed five. She was always surprised by his strength; she had seen him do some crazy stuff when he was working out or fixing things.

Their attention was turned away from Asald's bulging muscles when the door swung open, soft music reached their ears. No one came out to greet them, Asald looked at them, shrugged and went up the steps.

The Inn was even more beautiful inside. She didn't know if it was the music or the paint color but as soon as they entered a feeling of calm and safety washed over her. Behind the counter was an ancient looking man, his fine silk pajamas seemed like odd business attire till he introduced himself as Mr. Sandman. How was this town not a year-round theme park? His slow speech and deep rumble were relaxing as they followed him to their rooms.

"We have very few rules here but they are important ones. Do not go into the cellar, the dragon who lives down there is a noisy fellow but he minds his business so I let him stay. The windows are never to be opened, even if you think you hear music, the banshees like to play with visitors and trust me you don't want to get involved with them. Lastly, the sprites and brownies are excellent housekeepers but they can be naughty. If you leave them some chocolates, they will usually leave you alone."

If anyone else had been speaking that would have taken less than two minutes. With his slow drawl, it had been almost ten. He turned to leave them at their doors when she noticed he wasn't wearing shoes, instead, he had a pair of thick socks on. "Oh, and if you should have trouble falling asleep call the desk, I have just the thing to help you." With a slight bow to them, he turned and went back downstairs.

"Oh my god guys, thank you so much for forcing me to come along. This place is amazing."

"I admit it is so much more than I expected as well. Get settled in and we'll leave for dinner at seven."

Sarah gave Asald a mock salute and unlocked her room with the real, iron key Mr. Sandman had given her. Like the rest of the Inn, her room was beautiful and comfortable looking. She was surprised to see a definite lack of technology. Hopefully, they wouldn't be in the room much, she wasn't sure she knew how to occupy herself without a T.V.

As soon as she closed the door she couldn't help but jog over and do a back flop onto the giant marshmallow mountain of a bed. The satin sheets were more luxurious than anything she had ever owned. She was grateful the Innkeeper took such great care to make sure they had the best sleep possible.

After a quick phone call to check in with Alex she closed her eyes and enjoyed the silence. She hadn't been alone in years; the lack of noise was surprisingly deafening.

A knock on the door broke her focus, "It's just me." Penny's face appeared upside down over hers. "You look comfortable, explains why you didn't realize what time it was."

"I can't leave now, the bed has accepted me as part of it and I don't want to move."

"Ladies, let's go. We're going to be late."

"I know you love your new bed but Asald is getting antsy so up you go."

With a heavy sigh, she raised her hands. Penny walked around the bed and yanked her up. "Okay, okay, let's go."

Three

A short drive back through town took them to a restaurant set back from the main road. The stonework of the building gave it a medieval feel. Large lanterns hanging every few feet put off a tremendous amount of heat from the flames within. They were greeted by a hostess wearing a corset dress made out of large scales. She would hate to see the alligator those must have come from.

Sitting around a large round table were three giant men, she had thought Asald was big but he was average sized compared to them. Smiles instantly transformed their faces as they saw them and jumped up to crush them each in hugs.

"Finally, we meet!" Two of the giants looked alike, she assumed they were the brothers Pascal and Toussaint. The third man was calmer, standing back watching everyone, it was safe to assume this was Aristide, the one who owned a bookstore.

"We're so glad you all finally came up here. This is the best week of the entire year so you are in for a real treat." The brothers held out chairs for Penny and Sarah to sit in.

"There is no seat for Sebastian, is he not coming?" Asald looked between the three friends curiously.

After a couple of odd looks between them, Aristide made an excuse that he had to work. You would think being the Chief of Police would let you take time off when you wanted to.

A waitress dressed like the hostess passed out menus and took their drink orders. After ordering, Sarah excused herself to the restroom. At the back of the restaurant, her attention was caught by voices coming from behind a partition.

Always more curious than she should be she peeked behind the temporary barrier.

She had never seen such beauty before, the man sitting at a table deep in conversation stole her breath away. Tiny silver lines crisscrossed every inch of skin she could see. They shined with his movement, it was a beautiful sight.

She must have gasped, his head turned sharply and their eyes met. Seeing his face filled with anger didn't penetrate her thoughts as his beauty sent a shiver down her spine. Her fingers itched to trace the tiny scars running across his forehead and cheeks.

"Ma'am, may I help you with something?" Her transfixion was broken by the deeply tan man with black piercing eyes standing next to her in the hallway. "That is a private party, can I help you find your way back to your table?"

"Oh, I'm sorry, I was actually looking for the restroom."

"You are in luck; one more left turn and you will be at your destination."

Embarrassed at being caught she nodded and scurried away without a backward glance at the man who was sure to take over her every thought. Deep in her stomach, she felt a burning need to know who he was and what happened to him.

***

"Dinner was amazing, the charring on my steak was perfect." Asald leaned back and rubbed his still completely flat stomach.

"I agree, the smoky flavor of my chicken was excellent." Pascal set his napkin aside and waved over the waitress. "Can you let Pietr know we are ready for dessert."

Sarah's plate was removed as she spied the dark stranger from the hallway approaching their table.

"Pietr, so good to see you again. Did you enjoy that book I sent over last week?" Aristide talked more animatedly than he had all evening, it was obvious books brought him to life.

"Thank you for finding that for me, it is definitely a rare treasure." Intense black eyes found hers and smiled. "I see you found your way back to your party?"

Sarah couldn't help the blush she felt burning her cheeks.

"I heard you all are ready for dessert, allow me." Pietr leaned in and removed the center of the table which turned out to be a cover for a large burner. With a cheeky smile and a wink to Penny, he put his hands to his mouth and blew fire into the burner igniting it immediately.

Penny grabbed Sarah's arm as they both let out a gasp. "How did you do that?" Sarah couldn't help but laugh with excitement and intrigue.

"A little dragon fire to make your dessert more luscious." With another wink and a small bow, she watched as he went to the back and disappeared behind the temporary wall.

What she wouldn't give to follow him and see the sexy stranger again.

"That was incredible, how did he do it?" All four men at the table shrugged, fat lot of good they were.

Waitresses brought a pot of chocolate and skewers for everyone. A few minutes later trays of fruit, marshmallows, and small square cakes were set around the table.

She watched as Toussaint speared a marshmallow and held it over the flame browning it before dipping it in the melted chocolate. Asald grabbed a giant strawberry and dunked it completely in the chocolate before shoving it all the way in his mouth.

If she wanted to experience the moans echoing around the table she had to dive in before it was all gone. She selected an orange segment and covered it in chocolate, intense flavor burst in her mouth as soon as it touched her tongue. The sweet chocolate mixed with the tart flavor of the orange was unexpectedly delicious.

Less than ten minutes later the trays were empty and the chocolate bowl was wiped clean. With one last groan of ecstasy she sat back, for a fleeting second, she imagined unbuttoning her pants for a little relief.

"That was amazing, thank you for picking this place." Penny licked the last drops of chocolate off her fingers.

"It's the best place in town, I always think it's weird to eat at the mermaid's place. Their specialty is fish and chips and that is just too cannibalistic for me." Toussaint laughed hysterically.

"You all do take this paranormal stuff seriously don't you?"

"It's a lifestyle." Pascal winked at Asald before erupting in laughter.

"So, what are your plans tomorrow?" Aristide ever the somber one asked with a more serious tone.

"Besides exploring more of the city, we have to get our costumes for the ball Saturday night."

"That's right, it's imperative that you dress to impress. You must go to Seraphine's Disguise. She has the best shop in town and has a knack for picking the perfect costume to match the monster that is inside you." Toussaint wiggled his eyebrows at them before laughing again. They really were a merry band of brothers.

"If you guys want to meet up tomorrow give us a call." Aristide hugged each of them before leading them out of the restaurant.

She couldn't help looking back one last time at the partition hiding the private party.

She was surprised to see Pietr talking with someone behind the barrier, he turned and stared directly at her while he continued to talk. With another blush at being caught, she took off after the rest of the group. How will she ever sleep tonight with visions of that beautiful stranger haunting her thoughts?

Four

A soft knock on her hotel room door woke her from a dream starring the scarred stranger walking away from her while she cried. The intensity of the emotions reverberated through her body as she sat up.

"Sarah, are you awake?" Penny's soft voice came through the door.

"Just a second." She grabbed her cell phone, confused why her alarm was set to go off an hour ago but never did.

Not being a morning person, she dragged her feet to the door and opened it.

"Oh my god, what did you do to your hair?"

Confused, she reached up and gave her an equally perplexed look. Penny followed her as she rushed into the bathroom to check the mirror. She scowled as Penny continued to laugh at her. Tiny knots and braids took up every part of her head.

"How in the hell did this happen? She swore when she went to sleep last night her hair was not like this.

"Maybe the brownies and sprites didn't like you coming back with chocolate breath and none for them?" She held her stomach as she gasped for air between howls of laughter.

"You did this, didn't you? Did the Innkeeper let you in?"

Her hands flew up in a defensive pose. "Don't look at me, I never came in here. Maybe you drank more than you thought at dinner last night? Let me tell Asald we need a few minutes."

In utter shock and confusion, Sarah turned back to the mirror and attempted to start unraveling her hair, cursing at Penny for laughing her way out of my room.

"Good news, Asald said there is a hairdresser in town. If I remember correctly, you haven't done anything besides a basic haircut in years. How about we let them take care of this rat's nest and maybe throw some color in there too?"

"I don't know how you did this but I will get you back."

"I swear, I had nothing to do with this."

"Riddle me this, if it was the brownies why didn't they mess with you guys?"

"That's easy, we left chocolate kisses on the dresser." Penny winked at Sarah's astonished face and tossed something at her. "Take this and meet me downstairs when you are dressed." She caught the knit cap and laid it on the counter.

"Fine, you win, give me fifteen minutes."

She stuck her tongue out at Penny's retreating back while she contemplated retribution. She didn't know why Penny couldn't be like a normal friend and just tell her she looked like crap and needed a makeover.

***

"Seriously?" Sarah rolled her eyes as they stood outside the hair salon.

"Well, I guess it makes sense she would know a lot about hair."

"This town is so weird." She shook her head as they walked inside.

"Welcome to Medusa's Locks, can I help you?"

"I had a little mishap last night and was hoping you could rescue me."

"And she'd like some color added too." Sarah gave Penny a side eye before smiling at the young girl wearing an aqua colored wrap around her head, the color made her eyes stand out, almost hypnotically large and beautiful.

"Come sit down and let me see what we have to work with."

With a resigned sigh, Sarah sat down and pulled the cap off her head. She gave the girl credit, she didn't laugh. "Oh, you poor thing, I suppose you are at the Inn. Didn't they warn you to leave chocolates out?"

Sarah couldn't help the exasperated look she gave the girl. "Yes, he did but I know it was a joke."

"Of course, it was." She smiled and got started on the back of her head. "Sit back and relax, this is going to take a while.

Five

Sarah saw the woman in the mirror but she was afraid to believe who it was. This woman was beautiful, she was younger than her and looked carefree and confident.

How was it possible a simple haircut and color could alter her so much? She was on autopilot trying to survive for so long she hadn't realized she had drab, lifeless hair which prematurely aged her.

Her stylist, Meddie stared at her with a huge smile on her face, "You look amazing, do you love it?"

Speechless, Sarah let the tears fall. She thought they were tears of relief, maybe she had stopped dating because she had stopped believing in herself as a woman?

"Sweetie, don't cry, if you don't like it we can change it." She felt bad Meddie was looking around wildly for someone to help her with the crazy lady in her chair.

Penny and Asald chose that moment to return from their walk down Main Street.

Penny's eyes filled with tears, it's obvious she saw the same thing Sarah did.

"I was just telling her we can change it, you tell me what you don't like and I will fix it."

"It is perfect, don't change a thing." Penny ran her fingers through Sarah's auburn and eggplant striped hair.

Meddie had taken a good eight inches off, and her curls had returned, she'd forgotten she'd had those. "You are a genius, it's perfect." Penny's hands came down and squeezed her shoulders, her face serious again. "What do you think?"

Overwhelmed by all of the emotions she felt the need to break the tension. "I look hot."

Meddie's face transformed into utter relief as Penny laughed.

Meddie led them to the register at the front. Sarah tipped her generously then grabbed her in a hug, an odd gesture for someone like her who wasn't comfortable being touched. She needed Meddie to understand what she gave back to her.

Asald opened the door, smiling as Sarah passed by. "I'm glad I'm here to act as a chaperone this weekend, I'm going to have to fight the wolves off with a stick."

His words caused her stomach to do a flip. Was she actually excited at the idea of meeting guys at the party? Almost as fast as that thought came it was replaced by the scarred man. A very large part of her prayed he would be at the party tomorrow night. Maybe between her new-found confidence and whatever costume, she was wearing she would be able to talk to him.

"Where to next ladies?"

"Time to go shopping, of course, it's time we meet the mysterious Seraphine don't you think?"

Six

Commotion across the street from the salon drew their attention. A large group of men were on ladders hanging giant white sheets. Speakers were being set up throughout the park.

The sun was blocked from her face by the tallest man she had ever seen. Hair covered almost every inch of his body, it's fine white strands moved gently with the breeze.

"Let me guess, chocolate chip cookie dough?" Sarah felt her jaw open and close a couple of times but no sound came out. "You look like mint chocolate chip and you big guy are definitely a brownie sundae kind of man." His excited, expectant face looked back and forth between each of them.

"That's incredible, how did you know my favorite ice cream?" Penny's huge grin showed how surprised she was by his parlor trick.

"I'm Saroj, I own the ice cream shop over there." Sarah's eyes followed his long, hairy arm as he pointed to a cute store next to the salon. "Here's a couple of coupons, why don't you stop by later before you settle in your seats?"

Asald grabbed the slips of paper and turned back towards the men working in the square. "The seats you are referring to have something to do with this?"

"I guess you guys are new in town. It's a tradition around here to gather in the square and watch those really cheesy, scary movies the Friday before Halloween. Are you guys staying at the Inn?"

"Yes, we got in last night and we're staying through Sunday."

"I know Sandy keeps extra chairs and stuff for guests, so borrow some from him then come back here to set up. People start staking out the prime spots around five so don't be late."

"Thanks for the info, we'll definitely be back and I will be back for that brownie sundae." Sarah didn't think Asald realized he rubbed his stomach as he said this.

Their new giant, hairy friend waved goodbye and walked toward his shop, stopping and saying hi to everyone he passed.

"This town is full of surprises. I can never bring Alex here or he will demand we move immediately."

"I don't blame him, I'm kind of loving it too." Penny wrapped her arms around Asald's waist and squeezed.

"Let's not make any life-changing decisions after only one day. Now, let's go get you a sexy costume." Asald smacked her ass before grabbing her hand and pulling her down the street. Sarah couldn't help the huge sigh she heard escape; she hoped she would find a love like theirs one day.

Seven

"Welcome to Seraphine's Disguise, I am Seraphine." A woman, barely five feet tall and looking older than Mr. Sandman smiled at Asald and Penny. Her eyes landed on Sarah and her weathered face slackened. A shudder wracked Sarah's body, the woman's intense stare made her uncomfortable. The ancient woman shuffled closer and held her hands out towards Sarah. Unsure what to do she placed hers in the woman's much tinier ones.

"Oh my, this is an unexpected turn. I've wondered how long it would be but now I have my answer." She smiled as one hand reached up and cupped Sarah's cheek. "Perfect, you will be perfect."

She was so close Sarah could see every wrinkle etched on her tiny face. She couldn't help leaning in, she wasn't sure if she was imagining it but she wasn't, she had one emerald green eye and one violet eye. It took a pretty cool senior to wear colored contacts.

"What is your name my dear?"

"Sarah." The name barely came out, her throat had gone dry. She wasn't sure how much longer she could take the woman staring.

"What brings you to my store Sarah?"

"Um, well, they were invited to a costume party tomorrow night and I'm tagging along."

Her face transformed into excitement. "Perfect, this will be perfect. Come along, let's see what we have for you."

They followed along as Seraphine mumbled to herself as she pulled outfits off various racks. The store was packed but she didn't let this stop her. She paused in front of a young guy trying on a gold crown. "No, no, no Mr. Silver, that is all wrong. Here, this is for you." She handed the bewildered looking guy an Egyptian looking costume and shuffled on.

"Ma'am, would you like me to carry some of those?" Asald looked concerned at the pile of costumes Seraphine was building. Any more and she wouldn't be able to see over it.

"Do I look like an old woman to you? I've got this." She shook her head at him and grabbed another costume to add to the pile. "Okay, let's get started."

"You're up first handsome." She held the curtain open expectantly.

"Oh, sorry, I already have a costume. We're here for the ladies."

Her one green eye squinted at him, silently waiting for him to cave. It didn't take long before he cleared his throat nervously.

"Since I'm here, what's the harm in trying a few on."

Sarah and Penny shouldn't have laughed, it really was rude but how do you not when the first costume he walked out in was a court jester with tights and a pointy hat.

"This is not happening." Asald's pouty face only made them laugh harder.

"But baby, those tights are hot. I know what I'm getting you for Christmas." He shook his head and disappeared behind the curtain.

The next three costumes were equally as embarrassing. "It's a good thing you have another costume, none of these are going to work. Oh well, time for the ladies to try on some."

"You never intended to find me a costume, did you?"

Her devilish smirk said it all. A deep growl rumbled from him before he went back behind the curtain to change.

Back in his clothes he stomped out of the dressing area and sat on the couch they just vacated.

The first costume hanging up was a purple and black pirate costume.

"Um, I think you gave me the wrong size."

"I never get it wrong, let's have a look at you."

Sarah poked her head out of the curtain, "No really, there isn't enough material with this one."

Penny strutted out in a sexy Red Riding Hood costume, she had as little material as Sarah did but she was happily flaunting it. "Get your cute butt out here and let us see."

Seraphine's intimidating stare told her she was going to agree with Penny on this one.

With a deep breath, she stepped out and hugged her arms around her waist.

"Oh my god girl, I didn't know you were so sexy!" Penny's eyes lit up with excitement.

"I am not wearing this, if I pull it up to cover my boobs my ass sticks out but if I yank it down you can see my nipples." With a hand covering her cleavage, she backed into her changing room and took the outfit off quickly. The next two outfits were as tiny as the first one. "Oh, come on, if Walt Disney could see what they'd done with their Minnie Mouse costume." Sarah shook her head at her reflection, "Of course, if she had worn this maybe she and Mickey would have had kids by now." She muttered to herself.

"You can't say something like that and not let us see." Sarah heard the laughter in Penny's plea.

With her mouse ears still on she popped her head out from behind the curtain. "Seraphine please, you have to have something a little less revealing?"

She shrugged and grabbed a costume she just happened to have hanging over the back of her chair. "Perhaps this will make you more comfortable."

After a quick-change Sarah sighed with relief, she might not get a guy's attention wearing this but lord knows she would be able to relax and have fun. "This is perfect, I'll take it."

With a flourish, she threw back the curtain. Penny's bulging eyes and open mouth were clear indicators she did not approve of my choice.

"You can't possibly want to wear that, no offense Seraphine but that is horrendous.

Asald, say something, she just had her hair done all pretty too."

"Don't get me involved in this, this is her first night out in years and if this is what she needs to wear to have a good time than I say so be it."

The mirror across the room caught her eye. "It's not all that terrible Penny, stop being so pouty." She could admit the mad scientist look wasn't something a normal single girl would want to wear but there was nothing normal about her. The white lab coat and steampunk goggles gave her a sense of security. She wouldn't admit it out loud but she needed them to hide behind if she got nervous.

"Alright then, let's check out."

"Um, excuse me, Ms. Seraphine." The shy looking man from before was nervously standing off to the side.

"Yes Silver, what is it dear?"

"I appreciate your help finding me a place to stay and inviting me to this party but I can't possibly wear this."

Sarah could relate, he had the same look she did. Obviously, whatever she gave him was more revealing than he would like.

Her wrinkled hand came up and she waved him down towards her. She turned that intense stare fully on him. "I am never wrong, trust that I am doing what is best for you. Now let's get you out of here, Adam is waiting for you at his apartment."

Obviously, he couldn't resist her gaze either as he nodded and headed towards the register too.

"Don't worry my dears, everything is going to be perfect."

There she goes again, she had to be the most optimistic person Sarah had ever met. For her love life's sake, she hoped Seraphine was right.

Eight

"Popcorn for Penny and Milk Duds for Sarah." Asald handed each woman their treats and sat in the camping chair next to them.

"I'm glad the Inn had extra chairs, this would have been really uncomfortable on the ground." Penny wiggled deeper into her chair and snuggled under the blanket she borrowed off her hotel bed.

A shimmer to her left pulled Sarah's attention from the screen. The stranger from the other night with the scars covering his body was walking with the man from the costume shop earlier. Her mystery man had a hoodie pulled far enough forward it covered most of his face, but she still knew it was him. A moment of regret sliced through her, if she had introduced herself to the man at the shop it would have given her an excuse to speak to him again.

Her eyes never left his back as she watched them set up their chairs nearby and head towards the impromptu snack tent. "You know what, I'm not feeling chocolate. I'm going to go get some Twizzlers."

"I can go if you would like?" Asald started to pull himself out of the chair.

"I asked for the wrong thing, you shouldn't have to go again. Besides, I know how much you want to watch this movie."

Asald's dimples popped as a look of excitement crossed his face, "I haven't heard of this one before, I can't wait to see what a Creature from the Black Lagoon looks like? And where is this Black Lagoon?"

Sarah chuckled as she watched Penny pat his hand as she stood to leave. He had an innocence about him that was endearing and his curiosity was near insatiable. One day she was going to get him to tell her about his childhood, he had a lot of oddities that she was dying to understand but out of respect for Penny, she didn't pry.

They were quite used to him interrupting movies and shows to ask hundreds of questions. If it weren't for her being a mother she may not have had the patience.

A group of girls dressed like fairies were heading fast for the tent too, Sarah sped up to beat the girls in line. Now that she was less than two feet from the stranger that had been consuming her thoughts she was suddenly panicked and unsure of herself.

"I'm telling you, every time I collect teeth from that house they are all rotten. I'm tempted to stop paying for them." The girls' tiny gossamer wings fluttered in the breeze.

The strange conversation from the fairies behind her helped distract her chaotic emotions.

With only one group to go before the stranger got to the counter Sarah knew she was losing her opportunity. "Excuse me, I think I saw you at Seraphine's this morning?" Sarah tapped lightly on the man's shoulder.

Both men turned, suddenly any nerve she had built up disappeared. If she had any hope of making it out of there without looking like a complete fool she would have to try to ignore the scarred man staring intently at her. "I think you were struggling with the costume choices as much as I was." She laughed nervously. "I'm Sarah, visiting here for the first time."

The man from the shop reached out his hand, "My names Silver, I just moved here so that may make me a little crazier than you." Sarah shook hands with him then looked towards the ground awkwardly.

"This is Adam, he is letting me stay with him until I get my own place." Sarah's stomach squirmed, it was time to look into the eyes that have been haunting her impure thoughts for two days.

She wasn't disappointed, his grey eyes were staring through her and into her soul. A shiver ran down her spine, if she didn't know better she would have thought she might have just had a small orgasm. Can you come just from a look?

Up close the lines wove across his skin and entwined with each other beautifully.

Whatever had happened to him must have been horrible but in her eyes, it didn't do anything to detract from his looks. If anything, he was possibly the most gorgeous man she had ever met.

That last thought sobered her, even with her new haircut she wasn't attractive enough to be with him. She stared at his outstretched hand for a brief second before clearing her throat and looking back at Silver. "How silly of me, I forgot my wallet." She turned and rushed back to her chair. She heard one of them offer to buy her snack, like a coward she chose to run and hide instead.

Nine

The movie was probably great, Sarah wouldn't know. Her awareness never left Adam, she knew exactly where he was sitting and how many times he'd glanced her way. She wasn't egotistical enough to get her hopes up but butterflies definitely fluttered in her belly.

"Sarah do you want to go?" Sarah blinked and noticed Pascal and Toussaint had joined them at some point and all eyes were on her.

"We're heading over to Stoney's bar to have a drink with Sebastian." Pascal held his hand out to help her stand. "Join us and meet the fourth musketeer?"

"Sure, I can't tell you the last time I went out for fun on a Friday night that didn't include an animated movie and pizza."

"And it looks like our party just got bigger." Toussaint smiled at someone behind her.

The hair on the back of her neck stood, she knew who was there.

She turned slowly and smiled at Aristide who was being followed by Adam and Silver.

Oh goody, the panty wetting torture was going to continue. She hoped it was dark enough no one would see how red her cheeks were. Sarah folded up her chair and thanked Asald as he scooped everything into one giant arm.

"Lead the way." Penny smiled excitedly. Sarah knew Penny was in heaven with all these men around. She was probably calculating each man's worth and deciding who the lucky guy would be to get sucked into her machinations.

It was a short walk to the bar and every cell in Sarah's body was thrumming with excitement at having Adam so close. Her back was aching by the time they made it to the bar, she had been so stressed knowing he was walking behind her she had kept her posture ramrod straight.

Stoney's wasn't what she expected, she had assumed the name was more about getting high. Instead, the inside was dark, the walls were stone with real fire sconces all around. In each corner, a stone gargoyle statue sat staring at the crowd. The music was loud and people were dancing in the center of the room.

A large man in the far corner stood and waved them over, it wasn't hard to tell he was the fourth musketeer, his muscles were equally as large as the other men's plus the Sheriff badge might have given it away.

Sarah was surprised at the warm hug he gave her and Penny and the terse greeting to Asald. Maybe he didn't have to work the other night and chose to skip dinner because of Asald? How anyone could dislike him though was a mystery to her.

As soon as drinks were ordered Pascal and Toussaint stood and pulled them out of their seats, "Let's go ladies, there's no time for sitting."

Pascal winked at them before dragging Sarah unwillingly towards the center of the floor. She was not surprised to see Penny dancing her way towards them, Sarah was envious of her complete confidence in herself.

Sarah glanced towards the table and instantly regretted it, Adam was glowering their way. Every time she saw him the beauty of his scars awed her. It actually pained her to not go to him, something inside her desperately wanted to be with him. The intensity of the foreign feeling was both scary and exciting.

Pascal's hand wrapped around her waist and sent her spinning, she couldn't help the giggle that slipped from her mouth. The music was loud, the dancing was good and soon Sarah was lost in the euphoria of it all and danced as if she were alone in her living room.

Sweat rolled down her neck and slid between her breasts, she couldn't remember the last time she'd this much fun. Breathless and holding her side where a cramp had started she yelled to

Penny that she was going outside and slipped out for fresh air.

The cold night air instantly sent chills across her skin, it felt good now but she knew soon she would be freezing.

Taking in the much quieter atmosphere she leaned against the wall of the building and closed her eyes.

"I'm not sure you should be outside by yourself, this town may look innocent but we have our share of monsters too." Sarah shivered at the words spoken, not because of what was said but because of the mouth that said them so quietly next to her. She knew when she opened her eyes Adam would be inches from her.

"I'm glad you're out here to protect me." Her eyes fluttered open and wasn't disappointed to see he was only a foot away. It would only take her leaning off the wall to be flush with his body. Did he feel the pulsing need reverberating between them or was it only one-sided?

"You ran off earlier, do you want to go for a walk and talk?"

Hell freaking yes she did but saying that made her sound easy. Instead, she cocked her head to the side, "How do I know you aren't one of the monsters?"

"I admit I am more monster than man but you are safe with me, everyone inside will vouch for me."

She bit her bottom lip for a split second before deciding, "I'll text Penny that we're walking over to the ice cream shop and they can meet us at the gazebo in a bit."

Adam nodded and waited as she sent her text. He couldn't see her screen so he missed Penny's emoji responses of a tongue, lips, water drops and a bed. Sarah knew exactly where her friend's mind was at. She sent back a halo emoji and slipped her phone into her back pocket.

"It looks like I'm all yours." She knew how that sounded and decided to see how it was received. She wasn't disappointed to see something stir in his eyes, she hoped it was desire or she was going to be an aching mess for weeks.

She was surprised when he held out his arm and waited for her to loop her arm through his. She'd only ever seen men do that in the movies.

Suddenly shy, she blushed as she slipped her hand into the bend of his arm. "Lead the way."

Ten

Sarah became alert as they walked, Adam was constantly scanning the area and it was making her jumpy. When they approached the ice cream shop he looked through the window at everyone inside before entering. Maybe the town was more dangerous than she knew?

As they entered everyone inside smiled and said hello to Adam. Neither had to speak a word as the giant man from this morning scooped ice creams and handed the cones to them.

"Saraj you never cease to amaze me; how did you know I changed my mind tonight?" Adam licked the ice cream, tingling ran down Sarah's spine.

"Adam my friend, you must know by now I am a master of my craft. I could sense your change in moods, it felt like a cookies and cream kind of night for you."

Adam handed over money for both of them and led her outside. As before he scanned the area as they walked towards the gazebo.

"So, do you know everyone in town?" Sarah sat on the bench and gazed around the square watching people pass by.

"I've lived here for a very long time, we all know each other well."

"Why do you watch everyone so closely than? It seems like you are looking for danger?" She was surprised to see his face turn red.

"I'm sorry, it's an old habit, I don't even realize I'm doing it." He kept his eyes on his ice cream, she knew he was trying to force himself to not look around.

She should have dropped it but she wanted to know more about it, he fascinated her and she wanted to know everything about him. "Why is it a habit if you know everyone?"

She watched as his jaw tensed, he looked like he was warring with himself. Finally, he turned towards her and looked directly into her eyes. "I know how I look, I scare children, and adults are repulsed by me. I have learned to keep to myself when strangers are around. I don't go out often but when I do I try to be aware of new people so I don't bother them. You are the first outsider I have spoken to in a long time. I was so angry when you first saw me in the restaurant, I thought I was hidden. But then you looked at me and saw past my scars, I didn't see any fear or disgust in your eyes."

Sarah felt the tears well in her eyes, the motherly side of her wanted to wrap him in her arms and tell him all the ways those other people were idiots. The other side of her, the woman who had escaped an abusive relationship and hadn't had sex in years was clawing to get her hands on him. She wanted to show him exactly how gorgeous he was, she would be glad to trace every scar with her tongue and see where the lines took her.

For the first time in a very long time, she was going to be impulsive and do something she had never done before. She grabbed her phone, sent devil horns and a bed to Penny then stood and walked to the trash can. She tossed her ice cream in and walked back to a very confused looking Adam.

Gathering the last of her courage she stood between his legs and ran her hands through his hair. She got lost in his eyes briefly before bending down and placing kisses on his forehead, cheeks and finally his mouth. She pulled his hair, tilting his head to the side and deepened the kiss. Their tongues touched hesitantly at first then turned more eager.

A cold drip on her leg cleared her mind. When Sarah finally pulled away she was surprised to see she was sitting on his lap and something rather large was pulsing against her thigh. Adam's ice cream was melting, it ran down his hand and dripped on to her legs. She dug into her pocket and pulled out the old iron hotel key and waved at him. "Maybe we should go clean up?"

Words weren't needed, his breathing was ragged, he nodded curtly and lifted her off his lap as he stood. His clean hand reached down and entwined his fingers with hers. He tossed the last of his cone in the trash and took off towards the hotel.

A brief second of inner doubt invaded her mind, was she insane, she didn't know this man. She quickly tamped down those utterly boring and responsible notions and quickened her pace to keep up with him. This was really happening, mama was gonna get her freak on.

Eleven

For the first time in her life Sarah was not going to be the serious, mature person she always acted like. She wanted to feel carefree and live in the moment. She slid the scarf from around her neck and hung it on the outside door handle of her room. She chuckled at the expression Penny was going to have when she saw it. Her best friend had begged her for years to let loose, Sarah knew this was crazier than Penny had meant but she would still be thrilled for her.

The only light in the room was coming from the bathroom, Sarah was grateful it wasn't very bright, she was nervous about undressing in front of him. It only took one look at Adam for her to see him staring in the same direction, she realized he probably felt the same way if not ten times worse.

"Do you want the light off?" She hoped he would say no. If she was finally going to get laid and by a man as gorgeous as he was she wanted to see every inch of him.

Part of her wanted to see if the scars really were everywhere. She desperately wanted to ask how he got them but she wanted him to volunteer the information on his own.

"No, it's okay, I'm good with it if you are." He glanced towards the bed nervously, it dawned on her he was probably as rusty as she was.

She grabbed his hand and pulled him to the bed, she reached behind her and unzipped her dress. The fabric made a whispering noise as it slid down her body and pooled at her feet. She was willing to make the first move so he wouldn't be so focused on her seeing him. His vulnerability brought out her daring side.

Her hands shook slightly as she reached up and untucked his shirt from his jeans. She stared into his eyes as she pulled it up and over his head.

His stomach muscles twitched as her hands gently brushed down his sides and around to unbutton his pants. In her peripheral vision, she could see the tiny silver lines did cover his torso but she was surprised they were flat, she couldn't feel them.

She finally broke eye contact to kiss down his neck to his chest and lower. She pulled his clothes down as she kneeled in front of him. Her hands stroked back up his legs and around his hips. She kissed around the throbbing cock jutting towards her till she could feel the tension and need radiating off of him. Her nails dug into his ass cheeks as she took him deep into her mouth. His hands tangled in her hair, the tingling of her scalp sent goosebumps across her body. It had been so long since she sucked on a man she forgot how much she enjoyed it. She loved knowing he was at her mercy, his pleasure was completely tied to her willingness to give it to him. The louder his moans were the wetter she grew, her breasts felt heavy and her nipples were painfully puckered and desperate for their own attention.

With a feral growl, she was pulled up and against him. His mouth crushed down on hers, his need was palpable. Another growl came from him, this one sounded frustrated instead. He had been trying to unhook her bra and couldn't get the hooks undone. She chuckled and reached back to do it for him.

He sat on the edge of the bed and grabbed both breasts in his hands. She had always been proud of her large chest, she leaned her head back and closed her eyes letting him take his time to explore them. His hot mouth clamped on to the tight bead of her nipple, desire exploded inside her, she bucked forward and held his head to her, he better be suffocating if he broke contact.

It didn't take long for need to overcome her, she kicked off her shoes and pushed her underwear down. Adam stood and waited as she climbed on to the bed and laid down.

He stood still for a few seconds looking down at her, "It's been so long, I'm worried I won't last very long."

His truthfulness was endearing, she grabbed his hand and dragged him on top of her, "I have all night, we can practice a few times."

For the first time since she met him he smiled, deep dimples creased his cheeks. The light returned to his eyes, she could feel the tension leaving him. She stared at him in awe, she couldn't believe anyone ever saw anything but beauty when they saw him.

She was going to shatter into a million pieces if he didn't get inside her soon. She pulled his mouth down to hers and poured all of her feelings into the kiss. She wanted it to be a night they would both remember forever.

Twelve

The faint light streaming in between the curtain windows pulled Sarah from her peaceful sleep. For a brief moment, she forgot she wasn't alone and how brazen she had been the night before.

As if he knew she was awake a hand gently massaged her hip and slid across her stomach. The steel band of his arm pulled her against his chest, her eyes drifted closed as she felt the hair on his legs tickle the backs of hers, the heat from his body sending goose bumps across her flesh. Gentle kisses along the curve of her neck sent desire pooling between her legs.

Her confidence from last night was gone in the daylight. She wanted to make the next move but didn't know what it was. The realization that she would be back in her own bed the next night gave her all the motivation she needed to take things into her own hands.

She reached back, her fingers stroked up his thigh and in between them. Her hand wrapped around his already erect penis and squeezed firmly as she stroked him. His breathing grew ragged in her ear, his hot breath tickled her flush skin.

Her hand was pulled away as he pulled her over onto her back. She reveled in the weight of his body on top of hers, for a brief moment they stared into each other's eyes. Both could see the other was broken and needed to be loved for who they truly were. With one fluid motion, he slid deep inside her, her head rolled back with the depth of his thrust, his tongue traced a single drop of sweat down her throat to her collarbone.

Last night was frenzied as if both were afraid it would be over too quick. This was something altogether different, this is what people called making love, something she realized she hadn't had before.

Obviously, they weren't in love but both gave the other exactly what they needed to feel wanted and cherished. Maybe there was hope for them, maybe there was hope for reviving love.

Thirteen

Adam laid there staring at the ceiling, Sarah was draped across him, his fingers stroked along her spine. He was struggling to wrap his mind around the fact that he had a woman in bed, they were naked, and she could see all of him and wasn't disgusted. It had been at least seventy-five years since he slept with someone and that was a prostitute who had no issue doing him in the pitch black.

How did this stranger manage to pull him out of every protective layer he had wrapped around himself in less than forty-eight hours? She had gotten under his skin and for the first time in two hundred years, he wanted to get out of his house and spend time with her. From what he could tell she wasn't a witch so a love potion wasn't likely. He was starting to suspect she was his soul mate and he'd been going through the motions of life waiting for her to show up.

Panic was building in his chest, he knew this was going to end badly. She was a weekender who would disappear tomorrow night and now that she'd woken him up he would suffer in the loneliness that he hadn't realized surrounded him.

"Sarah, are you awake?" He didn't want to sneak out and be gone when she woke up but he needed space to clear his head too.

She yawned and flipped her head on his shoulder to face him. "Hhhmmm, how are you so bright-eyed right now? I feel like I could sleep the rest of the day."

Ego swelled in him slightly, he chose to believe she was exhausted from their multiple rounds of sex and not because she was on vacation.

"I have a project due today for a client, I need to get home. I didn't want you to think I took off on you." He could see the disappointment in her eyes at his announcement he was leaving, "I'll see you at the party tonight, right?"

She sat up, pulling the sheet up to cover her chest. "Yes, we're going to the party. Do you have time for breakfast at least before you go?"

Guilt was warring inside him but he knew he was getting attached fast and needed to get away for a bit. "I'm sorry, what if we meet at the buffet line tonight, it'll be like having dinner together?"

"Sounds good, thank you for last night, I had a great time." She leaned down and kissed his cheek before climbing out of bed and going to the restroom.

He felt like a piece of shit, but it was better this way in the end.

He got dressed and slipped out of the hotel room. He waved at Sandy as he left the building, the stoic man never had an expression on his face but this time he had the slightest smile curving his cheeks.

He hoped it was early enough the whole town wouldn't get to watch him do the walk of shame for the first time in his never-ending life.

Fourteen

Sarah stood in the shower letting the hot water beat on her back. The first time she had sex in four years and the guy takes off almost immediately. The many years of abuse she had suffered under her husband made it easy for her to slip into self-blame and thoughts of not being good enough.

She knew the feelings were wrong but it wasn't an easy habit to break. Penny's face popped into her head, her best friend would smack her right now if she knew what she was thinking.

With a sigh of resignation, she turned off the shower and got dressed. Her stomach was growling and she was never fun to be around if she hit the hangry stage.

She got dressed quickly and opened her door to knock on Penny and Asald's door. She wasn't surprised to find their door wide open, Penny had pulled a chair inside her room facing Sarah's door. She had the scarf Sarah had hung on her doorknob wrapped around her neck. The goofy smile on her best friend's face was mortifying enough but then Asald peaked around the door and smiled at her too. Sarah tried to step back in and close her door but their yells of protest had her stopping.

"If I come out do you promise to not pounce on me? Let me talk about it when I'm ready?" Sarah stared between the two of them, waiting for agreement.

Penny could see in Sarah's eyes that something was wrong. "Of course, forget we said anything. Let's go get breakfast."

Sarah watched as Asald leaned down and whispered to Penny, "Do I need to go beat some sense into that guy?"

Sarah chuckled and waved him off, "I promise he did nothing wrong. Let's drop it for now."

She turned down the hallway not looking back to see if they followed. Penny's hand slid into Sarah's and she squeezed. She could always count on her friend for knowing exactly how to comfort her.

"Aristide said there is an awesome bakery on Main Street called Magical Delights, we can get breakfast there." Asald held the door to the lobby open for them then led the way. As they walked through town Sarah still couldn't grasp the eccentricity of the place. She found herself daydreaming about living here with Adam, picturing Alex walking to school with a cauldron.

Thoughts of her son made her realize she slept with a man who didn't even know she was a single mother. She suddenly felt very reckless, that could be a deal breaker for some people. Then again, last night could have been a one-time event so she could be worrying for nothing.

Sarah could smell the sugar long before they got to the door of the bakery. There was so much pink and purple all over it looked like a five-year-old's princess party on steroids. The employee's behind the counter seemed to glow, their beauty was nearly blinding. The most unique part of them were the golden horn's jutting out of their foreheads.

"Ah, I get it, they're like unicorns." Penny's eyes danced with excitement. She dragged them to the counter pointing out everything as if they weren't seeing the same things.

Sarah had to admit their designs were creative, "If I eat any of this I may not fit into my costume tonight." Penny's head swung towards her, a perplexed look on her face.

"What are you talking about, there isn't an inch of skin showing on you and it's not form fitting at all. You need to lighten up and drown your last twenty- four hours in a sugar coma."

Sarah rolled her eyes at her, "I'm going to get a bagel and coffee." She leaned forward and ordered, they had bagels in every color of the rainbow, she wasn't sure that much dye was good for a person.

"Fine but we're coming back later for dessert," Penny grumbled before ordering her own bagel.

They sat at a table in the corner, Asald saw Toussaint walk by, "I'm going to say hi, I'll be back."

He wasn't four feet from them when Penny faced her straight on and quirked her eyebrow, waiting patiently.

Sarah took her time chewing, she stared around the cafe, taking in the sights while not looking in Penny's direction at all. Her eye's drilling into the side of her face finally became unbearable. "Fine, geez, you are persistent."

"What? I didn't say anything?" Penny batted her eyes innocently.

"What do you want me to say? It was amazing, he was a gentleman when he needed to be and aggressive when I wanted him to be. We had a great night, then when I woke up he seemed to shut down and said he had to go to work." She tried to not sound pouty.

"Don't read too much into that, he was totally into you last night and it was an unexpected date so maybe he really did have to work."

"Yeah, he was into me, three times actually." Penny choked on her coffee at Sarah's statement.

"Holy shit girl, lead with that next time!" Penny held her hand up for a high five, "I honestly didn't think it was going to get past some heavy petting, that was the freaking Olympics."

"It really was amazing, I'm pretty sure I orgasmed at least five times. He did things to me I had never even thought of." Sarah's cheeked burned in embarrassment. She knew Penny would never judge her but she still was shy admitting it.

Asald came back in, "Are you guys done yet? Toussaint offered to take us on a tour of the town."

Toussaint stood in the window of the bakery waving to them. "Sure, we have a couple of hours to kill before we need to start getting ready for the party." A horned employee appeared next to them and took their trash away, even the workers smelled like sugar.

Asald held the door open, "Let's go see what else this crazy town has to offer."

Fifteen

"I still can't believe you are going in that crazy costume, you have a cute butt under that lab coat and should be showing it off." Penny lectured Sarah for the tenth time since they dressed for the party.

"I know we don't know Seraphine well but something tells me you don't go against her wishes. And like I said before, I need the extra yards of material to let me hide behind if I get nervous." Sarah stuck her tongue out at her best friend and left her hotel room to go meet Asald at the car.

It was her first time laying eyes on him in costume and she was in awe. He stood leaning against the car, giant wings were folded up against his back, his skin was grey and mottled looking. "You look awesome! Your wings look so real." Sarah reached forward to touch them as Asald stepped back and climbed into the car, she was impressed how easily he got in with them on.

Penny came bouncing out of the hotel in her skimpy fairy costume. Her wings were nice but nowhere near as good quality as Asald's were.

They drove the short distance to the mansion on the edge of town. The gates were huge, ornate, wrought iron, two massive gargoyle statues stood sentry on either side. Asald pulled up to the gate, a call box was nowhere to be seen. After a few seconds, the gargoyle on the left started to stretch and turn its head towards the car.

"Get the fuck out, I give up, we have to move here." Penny was leaning in front of Asald watching the statue move.

"Good evening, may I help you?" All three were taken aback when the Gargoyle spoke to them.

Asald cleared his throat, "Um, we're here for the party." Sarah was very glad she was in the backseat, she would have been mortified talking to the stone creature.

"What's the password?" Penny jumped and threw herself against Asald, the gargoyle on her side of the car had leaned close to her window and spoken too.

"Did the guys give you a password?" Penny looked at Asald who shook his head no.

"We don't know the password but we were invited by Pascal and Toussaint. We met Seraphine yesterday, she would remember us and tell you we're allowed in." Asald hoped name dropping would help.

"I don't know Abenor what do you think, do we believe him?"

"He is dressed like one of us Larott, how could we turn him away?"

"Mistress doesn't like us letting people in who weren't invited. If they don't know the password, how do we know they're supposed to be here?"

'You know he's allowed, he's one of us. If he wants to bring along friends I say we let him in."

All three people in the car volleyed their heads back and forth watching the strange stone creatures arguing over the car at each other.

"Fine, I'll let you in but you have to do the password." Larott leaned close to Asald's face, laughter on his face.

"You do a password? I thought you said a password?" Penny looked perplexed.

"You must sing us a song to enter, it's Abenor's turn to choose."

Abenor's beady eyes squinted for a second while he thought, "Okay, this should be fun, I want you to sing I'm a little teapot and it doesn't count if you don't do the dance with it."

Sarah was nearly out of breath trying to keep her laughter silent. No way was she going to risk gaining their attention. Penny elbowed Asald and gestured for him to perform.

"This is ridiculous, fine, I'm a little teapot, short and stout," Asald growled the words out.

"Stop, stop, that is a fun song you are butchering and you definitely aren't dancing."

Asald glared at Abenor then let out a huff of irritation before starting again.

Sarah was impressed, his second try was much better, she still wouldn't let him sing it to a classroom full of kids but watching him tipping himself over, his arm shaped like a spout was too much fun to not laugh at.

"Larott, Abenor, how many times have you been told?" Both gargoyles snapped to attention, looking straight ahead rather than at the tiny woman who was standing on the other side of the gate.

Seraphine had appeared without anyone noticing, "I'm sorry for these two, they let the power get to their heads sometimes. While you do make an excellent teapot, I do suggest you come up to the house and join the party." She didn't wait for an answer she spun on her heel, took a few steps and was swallowed by the darkness.

The statues didn't say another word, the gates slid open silently. The winding drive ahead of them was ethereal. Like the rest of the town, the trees were barren yet beautiful. The light fog creeping across the ground, its whisps licking at the tires threatening to engulf their car.

Sarah was surprised Seraphine hadn't stayed on the road, she had vanished. "Every time I think I've gotten used to this town something like that happens. Can you imagine what those things must have cost? They were incredible, technology these days never ceases to amaze me."

A mile down the road the imposing mansion came into view. Judging by the looks on everyone's faces Sarah wasn't sure who was more impressed at the sight. "I want to thank you guys now for dragging me along, this is the coolest thing I've ever done."

Penny turned back and smiled at Sarah, I would say all in all this weekend has been awesome for all of us. Now, we need to go find your man so no stalling, let's go."

Penny calling Adam her man sent tingles through her belly, she realized how true she wanted those words to be. Penny was right, it was time to find him and see if this morning was a fluke or if he really did want to blow her off.

Sixteen

The gothic mansion was dark and gloomy on the outside, if it weren't for the buzz of people talking and music playing Sarah would have thought it was abandoned.

Asald parked the car and led the way, the large doors swung open slowly, a loud creaking echoing around the entryway. Asald was a tall man but even he looked tiny next to the doors.

The sounds of people partying led them to a huge ballroom. It was a Halloween party on steroids. Sarah couldn't believe her eyes, her mouth gaping open. She stood silently taking in everything around her. There were people who looked part human part werewolves and bears, a witch, a large yeti, and so much more.

"Excuse me." Sarah jumped as a pure white unicorn walked by, trying to get around their group. She reached out to touch it, she couldn't see any seams, but someone had to be inside since she heard it speak.

Penny grabbed her wrist, "You don't reach out and touch someone you don't know."

"I think I'm losing my mind, please tell me you heard that thing talk," She turned and pointed to a corner of the room, "and you see a freaking phoenix sitting on a table, right?" She spun the other direction and pointed to a group near them, "okay, come on, seriously? How the hell is there a satyr talking to Medusa and a dragon? They all look so real, I suddenly feel really cheap in my costume."

"No second guesses now, you were the one who said you had to follow Seraphine's orders." Penny reminded Sarah.

A loud, piercing whistle caught their attention, four gargoyles were standing across the room, two identical ones were waving exuberantly. "Is that Pascal and Toussaint?" Their wings were as impressive as Asald's, their skin was similarly colored but the angles to their faces and bodies were much sharper. "That must mean the other two are Aristide and Sebastian, did you guys plan to dress alike?" Sarah looked at Asald questioningly.

"Um, yeah, we thought it would be fun." Asald rubbed the back of his neck nervously before taking off toward the guys.

Sarah and Penny followed closely behind, they nearly ran into his back multiple times, they weren't able to pay attention to him when there were so many fascinating costumes around them.

They passed a table with a giant chocolate fountain flowing, tiny winged creatures were strewn all around it, some hanging out of the bowls with drool dripping from their open mouths.

"I guess the brownies over imbibed too soon, they are going to have serious chocolate hangovers tomorrow. At least we know they won't be messing with us while we sleep tonight." Asald shrugged and kept walking.

A shimmer at the corner of Sarah's vision had her head whipping around, Adam was standing next to a table talking to Silver. She thought it was funny Silver wore the Anubis costume Seraphine had been pushing at him, against his wishes too. Both men were gesturing towards a mummy nearby who looked angrily towards them.

Sarah didn't want to make the first move, if he was trying to get rid of her she wasn't going to look like an idiot begging for his attention.

She stood back from the gargoyle group, not really listening to their chatter, her attention focused on Adam and where he was. He was easy to spot, not only because his scars were brighter in the firelight but also because he wasn't in costume. Not that Sarah was complaining, his jeans were hugging his ass and his black t-shirt accented his muscular shoulders and arms.

When Sarah thought she was going to burst with the need to go to him he finally patted Silver's back and dragged him to their group. It took Adam a second to find her, being in the middle of five giant gargoyles she was hard to spot.

She was relieved he smiled and waved to her, she prayed that was a good sign. As he got closer he took in her costume, his facial expression getting gloomier by the second. She stayed quiet as the group greeted each other. Finally, his eyes met hers, a tingle ran down her spine.

"You're not in costume, you don't like these types of parties?" Sarah licked her suddenly dry lips, waiting for his response.

"I am my costume." Sarah was taken back by the tenseness in his voice. She didn't respond, she wasn't great at riddles and had no idea what he meant. Penny must have sensed her uncomfortableness and came to her rescue.

"I don't get it, what does that mean?"

"My name is Adam, I'm the monster that was created by Dr. Frankenstein. Brilliant at his work but his cosmetic surgery skills were lacking." His voice still had an edge to it. "And what are you?" His eyes hadn't left Sarah's, she was afraid to respond.

She finally cleared her throat, "I'm a mad scientist, I guess that means I created you?" She chuckled at her attempt at a joke.

"Awkward," Pascal whispered to the rest of the group.

"That was the worst time in my very long life and you decide to make fun of it?" Sarah could see the fire in his eyes.

Silver grabbed his shoulder, "You sound exactly like Cade did a few minutes ago, weren't you just telling me that he was being ridiculous?"

"It's not the same." He shrugged Silver's hand off of him, "I have to go." He nodded goodbye to everyone except Sarah, he didn't look at her again as he turned and left the room.

Confusion, Irritation, and embarrassment were coursing through Sarah, she didn't know which emotion was worse. Penny's arm wrapped around her shoulders and she pulled her close.

"Don't worry about him, I saw how he looked at you when he first came over. There is something there, give it time. From what I heard he's been a hermit for years, seeing him interact with you has been a shock to everyone."

"She's right, I've never seen him with a woman in all the time I've known him." Aristide hoping his words were comforting.

For a minute she stared at Adam's retreating back, she decided anger was going to win the battle. "You know what, this party is awesome, you guys are amazing. I'm going to forget about that drama for a while and have fun." Sarah said with steely determination.

Penny squeezed her shoulders, "Good for you, you deserve to let loose. What should we do first, Sebastian said there is an Arachne challenging people to a weaving contest or we can check out the Phoenix."

"I'm sorry to say I have no weaving skills, I'm not even talented at sewing buttons back on to clothes. Let's go check out the bird."

The group moved towards the area where cheers were erupting every few seconds. They got close to the table and found shot glasses were being lined up in front of the Phoenix, it was breathing fire across them, engulfing them in flames. "What can I serve you, we have Flaming B-52's, Bailey's Comets, and the crowd favorite Flaming Assholes but I doubt it's for the flavors as much as the guest maturity level." The Phoenix coughed, a small puff of smoke blew into their faces. "Excuse me, my throat's a little dry." It grabbed a lump of coal from a bag next to it and chewed on it while he waited for them to order.

Sarah had sidestepped till she was almost behind the bird and leaned in close to its back.

"What are you doing?" Penny asked in exasperation.

"How in the hell are they doing this? I can't see any wires and it's not a puppet." Sarah was inches from the bird.

"If he farts you are going to lose an eyebrow, get over here and grab a Flaming Asshole." Penny held a straw out towards her friend expectantly.

Sarah didn't want to admit out loud that the idea of sticking her face inches from a glass on fire scared her but she wasn't going to be the weakling either. She grabbed the straw and sucked as fast as she could. Her taste buds exploded, she recognized Creme de Menthe and a hint of Banana too.

"That's actually really good, I'll do another."

Seventeen

Sarah couldn't remember most of what had happened the night before but her throbbing head told her she had a good time. After her third shot, her memory was completely gone. A glance down at her body told her she had made it to her hotel room but that was it, her costume was still on.

A soft knock and her name being whispered were enough to send jabs of pain through her head. Penny came in with toast and a cup of coffee. "When I said to let loose last night, I did not expect the show you put on." She set the cup and plate on the table next to the bed and sat on the edge, "you aren't looking very hot, I assume you're pretty hung over?"

A grunt was all Sarah could muster, her mind still searching for any clue as to what she did last night.

"Why don't you go shower, I'll pack your stuff. Asald wants to get on the road as soon as we say goodbye to the guys." A sinking feeling landed in the pit of Sarah's stomach. If they were leaving quickly and Adam wasn't with the guys she wouldn't get to see him ever again. Even if he was being irrational last night she still had feelings for him and wanted to talk.

She took a few bites of toast before attempting to sit up. The food helped stabilize her enough to be able to talk. "All I remember is something about burning buttholes or something like that. Please tell me you kept an eye on me and I didn't do anything stupid?"

"First of all, it was flaming assholes not burning buttholes. Second, you had a whole group of gargoyles watching over you. You danced and had a good time, nothing to worry about. There was a vampire eyeing you but Sebastian got rid of him. I guess that's a perk of having the town Sheriff as a friend. Of course, it was priceless to see Toussaint and Pascal dragging you away from the werewolves. You kept yelling at them, demanding to know which one of them ate granny. When one of the werebears tried to get rid of you-you said something inappropriate about Goldilocks." Sarah was mortified, she didn't remember any of this.

Penny grabbed Sarah's hands and pulled her to a sitting position. "The hot water will do you good, now up you go before Asald starts his countdown."

"I want to see him try to tell me I have two minutes or he's leaving me," Sarah grumbled on her way to the bathroom.

Sarah stood under the water letting it run down her head, she always felt like water had some kind of healing power with her. When she finally felt human again she washed up and got out.

As promised Penny had packed up everything except an outfit and her toiletries, she had to give her friend credit she was efficient.

"If you go any slower Asald may come in here and carry you out." Penny smiled comfortingly, "He may be out there, everyone knows we're leaving."

Sarah nodded her head then looked down to meticulously study her shoelaces. She didn't want her best friend seeing the tears welling in her eyes. She knew Adam wasn't going to be out there and the thought crushed her. When she couldn't delay any longer she sighed and grabbed her suitcase.

"Okay, let's do this."

Eighteen

Asald stood next to his car, his head was thrown back laughing at something the twins were talking about. She couldn't hear them but given how exuberantly they were gesturing it must have been a good story.

Sarah was surprised to see Sebastian wasn't with the group, it was starting to bother her a bit. Aristide grabbed their suitcases and carried them to the trunk. She followed him, trying to get him alone. As she had hoped, Penny went straight to her husband's side.

"Aristide, I was wondering about Sebastian. He doesn't seem to like us and goes out of his way to avoid us, do you know why?" She saw his shoulders tense.

He glanced around the trunk to make sure no one was listening, "It's not all of you. He doesn't like Asald."

"That's crazy, there is nothing to dislike about him." She couldn't keep the incredulous look off her face.

"Between you and me, it's jealousy. He thinks Asald is too pretty to be one of us, he wasn't born into our kind. I say he can shift like us and fly like us so that is good enough for me."

"If you two are done Sarah needs to say goodbye to us too." Pascal's head popped around the trunk.

Sarah's mind was reeling, Aristide's words made no sense. This whole weekend made no sense. She was a sane, logical person but this town was getting to her. She was starting to think they had taken their lifestyle too far and they were starting to believe they really were the creatures they were pretending to be.

Aristide shut the trunk and rejoined the group. Sarah was engulfed in large arms, strong enough to crush her but gentle enough it made her want to melt into them. "I'm so glad you came along for the weekend, it was great meeting you. Asald and Penny have already promised to come back soon, you better be with them." Pascall squeezed her shoulders before Toussaint grabbed her and hugged the air out of her. No matter how crazy this place was she really did like these loveable goofballs.

She tried not to make it obvious she was constantly looking past their group, she couldn't give up hope that Adam was coming to say goodbye.

Once all the small talk was exhausted they couldn't put off leaving any longer. She knew everyone was aware of who she was waiting for.

Penny came over and put her arms around her shoulders, "Time to go." Sarah nodded, resigned she wasn't going to see Adam again.

Toussaint closed Sarah's door after she got in. "We can let everyone know it's safe to come out again, trouble is leaving town." Pascal doubled over at the look on Sarah's face. She truly was mortified to not know how out of control she had been the night before.

With a last wave at the guys, they drove through town and back home to reality. Black Hollow was amazing, she couldn't wait to tell everyone she knew about this amazing place but her heart broke a little knowing she was leaving a piece of herself behind.

Nineteen

Sarah had been home three days, Alex had run to her, jumping into her arms, a child's innocent love was enough to soothe any heartache she was suffering. He hadn't slept in her bed in a long time but she found herself letting him climb in so she wouldn't be alone in the dark thinking about Adam.

After work on the fourth day, she picked Alex up from after-school care. He was animated and excited to be leaving, they were having dinner at Penny and Asald's. "Do you think birdman will finally take me flying? Christian has gotten to go a bunch of times, I want to go."

"I think it's cute you still call Asald the birdman but we've talked about this, people can't fly." She smiled down at him as she brushed his hair out of his face.

"Yeah huh, I've seen him." His little eyes grew huge at something behind her. "Mommy look, that man looks like a baseball."

Sarah turned and found Adam standing a few feet away, she could see why Alex said he looked like a baseball, his scars did match the seams of a ball. She stood silent, in shock that he was actually here in the city. Other people had noticed him too, she was growing angry at their stares.

Adam ignored them, he only had eyes for her, she could see the uncertainty on his face. She wanted to let him keep guessing if she was mad for a few more seconds. He was wrong the night of the party, she hadn't meant any harm and he had attacked her for no reason.

His eyes slid down to the little boy holding her hand before looking back up at her, "I'm sorry, I didn't know you had a son. I should have called but the guys gave me Asald's address and he told me where to find you." He glanced down at Alex again, "I'll go, I'm sorry."

Her stomach dropped at the idea of him walking away, "Adam wait," She reached out and grabbed his arm. "Please don't leave." Sarah kneeled down next to Alex. "Alex, this is my friend Adam." The little boy held his hand out, waiting for Adam to shake it like Asald had taught him. Sarah's chest swelled with pride that he wasn't scared by Adam's scars, he was her grown up little man.

Adam kneeled down so he was eye to eye with Alex, he grabbed his hand firmly and shook it, "It is very nice to meet you."

"Mommy, can Adam come with us to Asald and Penny's?" He glanced up at Sarah.

"If he would like to have dinner with us he is welcome to."

Alex glanced back to Adam, "Aunt Penny makes the best macaroni and cheese, do you want to come with us?"

"Well if it's the best how can I say no?" Adam stood up, "As long as you are okay with it?" He waited for Sarah to nod. "I have my car, I'll follow you."

Butterflies danced in her belly, she put Alex in his booster seat and left. This was not how she expected her day to go. She was still in shock he not only left the relative safety of his town but also had been standing in broad daylight in front of strangers all to see her.

"I like him, mommy."

Sarah glanced at Alex in the rearview mirror, "I do to baby. I do too."

Twenty

Sarah sent a quick text to Penny letting her know Adam was in tow and staying for dinner. She got a text back with a GIF of a woman holding her hand across her forehead and passing out. Clearly, Penny was excited.

They pulled in the driveway, Adam stood awkwardly waiting for Sarah to get Alex out of the car. Penny and Asald were on the porch smiling stupidly at them.

Alex ran ahead, leaping through the air into Asald's arms. "Mommy brought a friend, come meet Adam," he leaned close to Asald's ear and whispered, "he is so cool, he looks like a baseball."

Sarah was mortified.

"I've met him, he is pretty cool." He set Alex down, "Christian is in his room playing, go inside and find him."

Before Sarah and Adam made it to the porch Penny held up her hand to stop them. "Dinner isn't ready yet, Sarah why don't you show Adam the lake out back."

She spun around and pulled Asald inside with her.

"Well, that was subtle." Sarah blushed at Adam, "It is pretty out there if you want to see it?"

He nodded and followed her, both quiet for the short walk to the water's edge. At first, neither spoke, they stared into the water contemplating their next words.

Adam broke first, "It didn't take me long to realize I had been an ass at the party. Every time I think I'm over what happened to me something brings it back up." He pulled her over to the bench facing the water and sat down. "Asald told me you don't know about us, I want to see where this is going with you but we can't move forward until you know the truth."

Sarah's face was hot, she knew deep down what he was going to tell her but the logical side of her brain was still fighting it.

"I was born in 1790 in Brussels, Belgium. In 1818 there was an accident and I was trampled by my horse. My mother should have let me stay dead but in her grief, she searched for a way to bring me back. She heard about an alchemist in Darmstadt, Germany who had been experimenting with bringing people back from the dead. Against my father's wishes, she took my body to his castle. He tried his best to put me back together but you can see his sewing skills weren't the greatest. It took a couple of tries but his experiment worked, I came back to life." Adam was staring at the water, oblivious to the look of confusion Sarah was giving him, "I don't remember the first couple of years, I had to be retrained as if born again an infant. Dr. Frankenstein had started calling me Adam in reference to Adam in the Bible, we were both the first of our kind. After my mother died I stayed with the doctor until his death a few years later. It didn't take long for me to see the biggest fault with what my mother did. I'm not able to age or die." His voice had turned bitter. Sarah could hear the pain and longing in his voice. "I was so lonely until I found Black Hollow, almost everyone there is immortal like me and accepted me without question."

Finally, his attention turned back to Sarah, she searched his eyes looking for the truth, "So you are trying to tell me everyone in Black Hollow is the creature they were pretending to be? It's not all for show?"

Adam nodded, she felt like she was going insane, did he actually expect her to believe that story? Her throat was constricting, she needed space. She stood and started backing towards the house, she could see the hurt in his eyes.

A flapping noise behind her had her spinning around. A creature with giant wings was descending from above the trees. Asald landed in front of her, he didn't say a word, his body shook as he morphed from a man into a stone gargoyle in front of her.

She wasn't ashamed to admit doing it, she screamed and took off running for the house. Penny was on the porch ready to catch her in her arms.

"He's a... he's a..." Sarah's eyes were bulging.

"Take a breath, yes, he's a gargoyle just like Pascal, Toussaint, Aristide, and Sebastian." Penny held Sarah's shoulders breathing deeply with her, trying to help her calm down. "I know this seems insane but it's the truth. Alex can tell you too, Asald is the one who saved us that day on the roof from Hank. We didn't do anything, Asald had shifted and fought him."

Asald walked up and stood next to them, she glanced over, relieved to see he looked like a normal human again.

"You know it's true, stop and think about everything you saw this past weekend, there is no other explanation for how real it all was." Penny dropped her arms and stood next to Asald.

"I need a few minutes, can you let me think for a second?" Sarah was trying to grasp everything she had been told but she was struggling with the idea that she had been in a room with a real dragon and mortified at the idea that she had flirted with the weretigers who apparently were real and could have eaten her and not in the way a woman wants to be eaten.

She shook her head at her inappropriately timed dirty thought. Asald waved Adam up to the house, she stood still while they went inside to give her space.

The last week replayed in her head, she thought back to everything she saw and heard. She did just see Asald drop out of the sky and turn into stone so she couldn't deny they were telling the truth but that would mean everything she had ever known about fairy tales and monsters was real and that thought was terrifying on its own.

She couldn't deny that everyone had been nice to her, she never felt unsafe. Asald was the reason both she and Alex were alive today and every cell in her body was screaming for her to accept Adam.

It wasn't going to be easy but she finally came to terms with what she had heard and decided to rejoin the group. As she walked inside she did the math and realized he had been alive over two hundred years, she wasn't sure she wanted to know how many women he had slept with in all that time. Not that she was an angel but she's had a lot less time to rack up the numbers either. She shrugged, that could explain how he was so good in bed.

Twenty-One

Dinner was quiet and somewhat tense. The conversation was mundane which helped ease Sarah's mind. The boys at the table were unaware of the tension in the room and thankfully provided plenty of entertainment to help move the night along.

Once dessert was done the boys were yawning and rubbing their eyes, "It looks like it's time for someone to get to bed." Sarah tussled Alex's hair.

"Can Adam carry me to the car?" Alex held his arms up expectantly.

Adam looked at her for permission before picking the boy up. He immediately laid his head on his shoulder and closed his eyes. Sarah wasn't sure if her heart exploded or it was her ovaries, he looked too damn good holding her child.

Penny linked arms with Sarah and walked her out, "I'm sorry we kept this from you for so long. It has taken Asald years to acclimate to our time and he wasn't sure if you would accept him."

"Tell him I still love him and will always be grateful for what he did for us?"

Penny nodded and hugged her best friend. "You deserve happiness, give Adam a chance."

Sarah waved to Asald who had stayed up on the porch holding Christian who was clearly as worn out as Alex was. Once Penny was out of earshot and Alex was buckled in Sarah walked around the car and stood by Adam.

"Would you like to follow me back to my apartment? We can keep talking?" Sarah was nervous to hear more but she had already decided there was no way she was walking away from him now.

"I would love nothing more, are you sure?" Sarah leaned up and kissed him, she hoped that was all the affirmation he needed.

Twenty-Two

Sarah sat at work replaying the night before, she had stayed up talking to Adam for hours. His stories comparing what it was like to live in different centuries fascinated her. She was jealous at the same time as grateful she wasn't alive during some of the worst periods in history.

He had told her more about his time after the rebirth as she liked to call it, her heart broke listening to his pain as he told her about watching everyone he had loved die. Living in Black Hollow had saved him in more ways than one, he was finally able to get close to people who weren't going to leave him after eighty years.

She knew he was shy to be around humans but hadn't grasped how deeply he tried to stay hidden from them. The fact that he not only left Black Hollow to come for her but also stood in broad daylight for anyone to see him had her falling head over heels for him.

She told him about Hank, the abuse, living in the shelter, and everything Penny and Asald had done for them. He was seething with anger at times during her story, he cursed her ex and the coward he was.

Their emotions had been running high, she had invited him into her bed, they made love while the sun slowly rose.

By morning she was exhausted and wanted to sleep but Alex was not going to understand mommy wanting to sleep the day away.

Adam had agreed to stay hidden in the bedroom till they were gone, she didn't want Alex asking questions about them she didn't have the answers to yet.

He was going to go home and on Friday she and Alex were going to Black Hollow. He was going to ask his roommate Silver to stay somewhere else for the weekend so they could stay in his spare bedroom.

She finally understood why Penny and Asald hadn't told her about his secret, she had no idea how to explain the town to Alex. Her best idea was to tell him it was all pretend like she had first thought then tell him the truth if things continued to progress with Adam like she hoped they would.

Now she had to make it through the next two days waiting to see him again.

Twenty-Three

Friday finally rolled around, Sarah wasn't sure who was more anxious to get on the road, her or Alex. Penny and Asald decided to take Christian and go back to the Inn too.

The night before they had told her his story. She struggled to comprehend he had been in hell, like the literal fire and brimstone hell you were taught about as a child in Sunday school. Her heart broke listening to him talk about the woman he had lost and what he had done to save her. She finally understood why Aristide had said Asald wasn't born one of them, he had been cursed and turned into a gargoyle, he had been born a human. It was all a total mind fuck she was still reeling from.

Sarah and Alex followed behind them in their car, as the trees started to turn dark and leafless Alex's eyes grew bigger. She couldn't wait for him to experience the people in the town, it was a paranormal Disney World.

At the turn for the Inn Asald's arm shot out the window and waved to them. Sarah drove straight and turned further down towards the address Adam had given her. She was surprised to find him sitting on the stoop waiting for them. His smile warmed her from her head to her toes. As soon as Alex's feet touched the pavement he ran for Adam and held his arms out for a hug. Adam wrapped in his arms and looked at her, the look on his face was priceless. He couldn't believe how easily the little boy had accepted him scars and all. The innocence of children never ceased to amaze her.

"Mommy your turn." Alex waited expectantly for the two secret lovers to hug. Sarah turned her face into his neck and took a deep breath. She lightly kissed the scar below his ear, a small shiver ran down his body.

"Someone's feeling naughty." He whispered into her ear before she pulled away. He had no idea how x rated her thoughts were at that moment, and every minute she thought about him. He had turned her into a walking hormone.

"Let's get you guys settled in then we can meet the group at Scales N' Tales." He grabbed her bag from her and waved her to go in first.

"What's unique about that place again?" Sarah had told Adam ahead of time that she hadn't told Alex the truth of the town yet.

"The mermaids run it, they serve mostly seafood." He smiled at the look of horror on her face.

Adam showed them around the apartment, there were antiques on every shelf, she had no doubt he had collected them over the years. His dining area had been turned into an office with four large computer monitors.

"Yeah, when you live alone you don't really need a formal eating area." He shrugged apologetically.

They dropped their bags in the spare room, she stole a glance at his bedroom, the huge, puffy bed was inviting. Alex was a very deep sleeper, she hoped they would be able to sneak some alone time in during the night.

"It's not a bad walk to the restaurant but we can drive if you'd prefer." He held his car keys up questioningly.

"After that many hours in the car, I think we could use the walk to stretch out our legs and burn off some energy." Her eyes flitted down at the boy dancing from foot to foot anxiously.

He led the way outside and down the road, the first building they came across was the school, "We're a small town so Kindergarten through Senior year go here." They turned the corner and passed the movie theater across from the library. Alex stared intently at all the interesting looking people in front of the theater. Most were dressed like the creatures they truly were, now that Sarah knew they were real she wanted to take her time studying them too.

As they passed Medusa's Locks and Yeti's Ice Cream shop the owners poked their heads out and waved to them. Sarah didn't realize how good it would feel to be a part of a community. In the city, you are lucky if you know even one of your neighbor's names. Here people went out of their way to be friendly to each other.

Many of these creatures would be feared if people knew they were real and yet it's those same humans who aren't half as decent as these so-called monsters were.

By the time they made it to the restaurant, Alex was bursting with excitement at everything he had seen. Sarah was relieved he was enjoying himself, she was quickly falling for the man and the town, having her son like them too would make everything easier.

Adam held the door open to let Sarah walk in first, as she stepped inside multiple people yelled her name. She was excited to see the whole gang was waiting for them. She had quickly come to think of these loveable gargoyles as her friends as well as Asald's.

She grabbed a seat next to Penny and introduced Alex to everyone.

Sarah studied the menu until the waitress came over to get their drink orders. Immediately Sarah forgot what she was going to order. The young woman was intoxicatingly beautiful. Her blonde hair hung to her waist and shimmered as if she were floating in water. Her skin was so pale blue it was almost see through. Now Sarah understood the stories about mermaids luring humans into the water.

Once the waitress had their order and was gone Sarah's head cleared from a fog she hadn't realized she was even in. What kind of powers did these merpeople have over humans?

"So, Sarah, I heard Chief Holland is having a party this weekend, want to go?" Pascal asked her innocently while the rest of the table burst into laughter. Penny looked as confused as she felt.

"Why is that so funny?"

Toussaint wiped the tears from his cheeks, "Because he's the Chief of the Fire Department and also the Phoenix from the party the other night."

Heat rushed Sarah's face, of course, they had to bring up her drinking. "Haha, very funny."

"Hi everyone," a trio of young women Sarah vaguely recognized walked up to their table. "I see you've come back to town and so soon, I guess you had fun?" The brunette leading the group looked at Asald, Penny, and Sarah expectantly.

"I invited Sarah to stay with me for the weekend. Asald and Penny came back to visit with the guys." Adam admitted freely to the girls, Sarah knew what his statement implied. It was a good thing her face was still warm from the group's teasing or she would have been blushing more.

"Well, you all seem like lovely people, I'm sure we'll see each other again soon." The group waved and went to sit at a nearby table.

"So, who are they?" Sarah asked Adam.

"The girl who did all the talking was Josephine, she's the town dentist and also a tooth fairy." He nodded at the look she gave him, "The other two are woodland fairies, they own the florist shop we passed by Yeti's."

Sarah didn't have words, she had started to accept all of this was real but that didn't mean it was any easier to grasp each time she learned something new. She studied them for a few seconds before remembering they had been behind her in the concession line during the movie the weekend before. She had heard them talking about collecting rotten teeth but Sarah had been so infatuated with Adam she hadn't really thought about what they were saying.

"A round of drinks, courtesy of the ladies in the corner." The waitress had returned, she set various concoctions around the table, not asking anyone which drink they wanted. Josephine and her two sidekicks waved at their group then held glasses up to salute them.

She could really get used to this town, everyone really did look out for each other.

Twenty-Four

After dinner, Sarah and Adam walked back to his apartment. Penny's desperation for them to get together had her begging Sarah to let Alex stay at the hotel with them for the night. Alex none the wiser to the adult undertones of the decision begged and she gave in. He would never turn down having a sleepover with Christian.

Along the way Sarah had stopped multiple times, exhaustion was overtaking her.

By the time they had reached his front door she was leaning heavily against Adam's side, "Maybe you should call Penny, something isn't right." Her eyes rolled back in her head and she crumpled. Luckily Adam caught her before she hit the ground. In a panic, he picked her up and ran to his room. He laid her gently on his bed and tried shaking her awake. She was breathing but he couldn't get her to open her eyes. He grabbed his phone and called the hotel. Sandy grudgingly agreed to risk waking his guests.

Adam paced the floor waiting for Penny or Asald to call him back, a minute later his phone buzzed. "Hello?"

"Adam, what's wrong?" Penny sounded anxious.

"I don't know, Sarah is unconscious, the last thing she said was for me to call you. Does she have a medical condition?" Adam tried to stay calm, his heart threatening to beat out of his chest.

"No, Sarah has no issues that I'm aware of. Let me tell Asald I'm leaving, I'll be there in five minutes." She hung up without another word.

Penny's lack of explanation scared Adam further. While he waited for her he contemplated calling the clinic. Dr. Jason Larson and his twin brother Dr. Jonathan Larson were the town doctors and vets, they also happened to be sphinx. They rarely treated humans but surely, they weren't that different than shifters and monsters like him. He knew Jonathan was out of town, he hoped Jason was around.

Adam heard the car door out front and ran to let Penny inside. She didn't say a word, rushed to her friend's side and inspected her the same as he had.

"She doesn't feel hot or cold, her breathing is shallow but other than that I don't see anything wrong. Is there a hospital I can take her to?" Penny chewed her nail anxiously.

"There's a hospital a few miles outside of town. We do have doctors that make house calls, I can try to get them?"

Penny nodded and went back to poking and prodding Sarah.

Adam dialed the number saved in his phone and paced waiting for his call to be answered. Fridays nights in this town were pretty lively, he just prayed the doc wasn't already three sheets to the wind.

On the sixth ring, his prayers were answered, "Hello?"

"Dr. Larson, it's Adam, can you come to my apartment, I have someone staying with me who is ill and I don't know what to do."

"Of course, let me get my medical bag and I'll be right over."

"Thank you." Adam hit end on the phone without waiting for a response then tossed his phone next to the bed. "He'll be here soon."

Twenty-Five

"I'll be honest, a perplexed Dr. Larson said, I can't find anything wrong with her either. I'm going to take some blood samples back to the office and run some tests. You can take her to the hospital if you want but I don't think there is anything they can do differently. I can bring some monitoring equipment over and we'll watch her closely until we get the test results in then we'll make a decision?" He looked between Adam and Penny waiting for one of them to make the call.

"Sarah's not a big fan of hospitals so if you don't think she is in any immediate danger we can wait a little while." Penny brushed a tear from her cheek.

"Can you fill out as much of this paperwork as possible while I draw her blood? Any medical history you can give me will help." He handed her a couple of papers then turned to work on Sarah.

Penny wasn't sure if you would call it luck but she happened to know quite a bit of Sarah's history. She had reviewed all of it when Sarah and Alex came to the shelter.

Adam glanced at her multiple times, she couldn't help how long it was taking, Hank had been an asshole.

She finished the last page and handed it to the doctor who had been waiting patiently. He scanned the sheets and whistled. "That is a lot of broken bones."

"She was in an abusive marriage for a few years before she was able to escape." Penny glanced towards Adam then back to the doctor. She didn't know if Sarah had told him yet, she hoped Sarah would understand if she had just outed her.

Dr. Larson squeezed Penny's shoulder comfortingly and left the apartment. For a moment neither Adam or Penny said a word.

Finally, Adam walked over and brushed the hair from Sarah's forehead. "She told me about her ex but she didn't give much detail. By the amount of writing you did and the doc's reaction I'm guessing it was much worse than she made it out to be."

Penny could see the anger radiating off of him, she was glad to see he was able to control it. Maybe after being alive a couple of hundred years you get good at managing emotions. "I know it's not right to say but part of me wishes Hank had died that day on the roof, jail is too good for him." Penny cleared her throat, she wasn't as good at controlling her emotions as he was. "I'm going to call Asald and update him. Is it okay if I sleep here, I want to be close in case," she stopped, she didn't want to finish the sentence.

She grabbed her cell phone and went to the kitchen. All she wanted was Asald to be by her side comforting her but she knew he was going to have to be there for Alex and keep him entertained so he didn't know anything was wrong. She was not going to worry him if she didn't have to. They had been through enough already, Penny would be damned if she would bring that little boy any more heartache.

Twenty-Six

Seven restless hours later Adam and Penny were both sitting anxiously by Sarah's side waiting for Dr. Larson. He had called saying he was stopping by, Adam hoped that meant he had news.

The quiet beeping of the machines monitoring her heart and blood pressure was starting to make his skin crawl. He needed her to wake up, he couldn't take losing another person he loved.

A knock on the door had Adam jumping up and letting Dr. Larson in with a fiery Seraphine hot on his tail. She ignored everyone as she went over and touched Sarah's forehead, she closed her eyes concentrating on something no one else could see or hear.

"Most of the tests have come back and I'm sorry to say I'm not finding anything specific. Her kidneys are starting to struggle and I can already see she is starting to turn blue around her lips. That usually means her red blood cells aren't getting enough oxygen. I'd like to move her to the clinic, she'll be closer to the rest of my equipment in case she needs it and I am going to start widening my tests to look for more rare conditions."

"There is darkness around her." Everyone turned to see Seraphine had opened her eyes again, "I think someone did something maliciously to her. You need to stop looking for natural explanations."

Dr. Larson stared at Sarah for a minute, "I will include poisons and drugs in my next round of tests. I wouldn't have even thought it could be something like that. We've never had a visitor intentionally harmed, you should let the Sheriff know." He waited for Seraphine to nod before turning to Adam. "Let's get her to the clinic, we don't know how fast she is going to continue to deteriorate."

Seraphine walked up to Adam and grabbed his hands, "Stay strong for her and she will return to you, have faith." She smiled at Penny then turned and left as quickly as she had come. Adam had known her for more than a century and he still couldn't get used to her all-knowing ways.

Chapter Twenty-Seven

They had been sitting at the clinic for three hours, Adam didn't know who was more anxious, him or Penny. Sarah didn't look any better, actually, her already shallow breathing was now coming out in short rapid breaths.

The machine next to the bed alarmed, the sound making both Penny and Adam jump. A nurse ran in, Dr. Larson followed quickly behind. "Step outside for a minute, let us see what is going on."

Adam had experienced a lot in his life but being asked to walk away at that moment was probably one of the most difficult requests he'd ever been given.

Penny grabbed his arm and pulled him into the hallway. "There is nothing we can do except get in the way, come on."

She sounded strong but Adam could see the tears rolling down her face. He didn't know her well but he knew how healing a hug was. He awkwardly pulled her close and let her cry on his shoulder. Before Sarah he hadn't hugged another person in years, now he's had contact with two people in the last week and both human. His life had certainly taken a turn, except now he felt like he was on the edge of a cliff and his ability to survive hinged on Sarah waking up.

Ten excruciating minutes later Dr. Larson joined them in the hallway, "We had to intubate her, she's starting to go into heart failure. We are running out of time, I'm going next store to talk to Seren."

Adam's throat felt like it had shut, the air was not making it to his lungs. Heart failure, how was this even possible?

"Who's Seren?" Penny stared at Dr. Larson's retreating back.

"He's the apothecary or a pharmacist, actually he's a wizard and much older than I am. Dr. Larson is smart to talk to him." Adam called over the nurse who had been working on Sarah, "Can you have someone get Alizon," he looked back at Penny, "she is the only residing witch in the area," he turned back to the nurse, "she may be able to help Seren and Dr. Larson."

The nurse nodded and went back to the desk. Adam and Penny cautiously walked back into Sarah's room, neither was ready for the site of her with a tube in her mouth.

"She doesn't deserve this, she's had enough bad in her life." Penny stroked the hair from Sarah's pale face.

A quiet knock on the door got their attention. Sebastian and Aristide stood staring at Sarah. "Seraphine called me. Does the doc really think this was intentional? That kind of stuff just doesn't happen around here." Sebastian's fingers tapped subconsciously on the handle of his gun.

"They don't really know what is causing this but she's getting worse by the hour." Adam's voice hitched. "Maybe we should bring Alex to see her?"

No one was thrilled with the idea of explaining the situation to the boy. "Let's give it a little more time, Pascal, Toussaint, and Asald took the boys flying, they have a whole day of fun planned. Alex won't even notice he hasn't seen his mom until later tonight." Adam appreciated Aristide's optimism.

"When she wakes up she is going to kill Asald." Adam looked questioningly at Penny, she shrugged, "she is extremely protective of Alex, when she finds out he went flying without her knowledge she is not going to be happy."

"Do you guys want to go get showers and food, we can sit here till you get back?" Sebastian offered.

"I don't think I can leave her." Adam nodded at Penny's statement, he agreed completely.

"How about this, Adam come with me to the bakery, we'll grab some food and bring it back." Adam started shaking his head at Aristide's offer,

"You need the fresh air, come on, clear your head for a few minutes."

Aristide grabbed his arm and dragged him out, his stomach decided at that moment to be a traitor and growl loudly. Aristide gave him a knowing look as they crossed the street.

They ordered quickly, Adam tapping his foot nervously as he waited for their order to be bagged. Out of the corner of his eye, he saw a commotion outside, dread filled him as he saw Dr. Larson running from the apothecary back to the clinic. He didn't wait, he took off at a dead run, only steps behind the doctor as he ran into Sarah's room. Sebastian was holding a sobbing Penny in his arms in the hall, he reached out and stopped Adam from going inside.

"Let me go!" Adam roared in anguish.

"There is nothing you can do." Adam tried to see Sarah but couldn't between the doctor and nurses working on her.

"What happened?" He couldn't pull his eyes from the room.

"Her heart stopped, the nurses were there in seconds. It's going to be fine." The confidence and strength in Sebastian's tone were the only things keeping Adam from falling to pieces.

Aristide walked up with the food in hand, Sebastian whispered the update to him, he squeezed Adam's shoulder, he knew his friend was trying to comfort him.

It was a long time before Dr. Larson came out, their group had sat in chairs across the hall, everyone jumped up as he approached.

"She's okay, I'm not going to lie, that was touch and go there for a few minutes. We're racing the clock, Seren and Alizon are meeting me in the lab. We're working as fast as we can but you need to prepare yourselves in case,"

Adam didn't wait for him to finish his sentence, he couldn't listen to him anymore.

When he reached the door, he was able to see her again and it broke him. Her eyes were sunken in, the blue had spread to most of her skin. He staggered to the bed and collapsed in the chair. He grabbed her cold hand and held it as he leaned on the bed, resting his forehead on the side of her face.

"I've tried to die, I wanted to leave this Earth so badly I tried killing myself more times than I can count." Tears fell from his face to hers. "You don't get to come into my life, give me hope and a reason to want to live then try to leave me. If you die, I want to die too but I can't. I'll be stuck here; the world will go on and I'll be alone again." Anger laced his words, "For a brief moment I actually thought I was going to find love, for the first time I pictured being a father to that amazing little boy who is waiting for you to wake up." His voice had risen, someone's hand touched his shoulder trying to pull him back, he jerked away, this was his confessional and she was going to listen to every last word he had. "I've tried giving up so many times, I didn't have anyone begging me to stay but that's what I'm doing now. I'm begging you to fight, to come back to me, and to Alex. It took two centuries for me to find you, I'm not giving you up already. I don't know how to live if

I lose you, I need you to come back to me." He ended in a whisper, despair still clear in his voice.

The room stayed silent except for the beeping of the machines. Adam didn't look around, he stayed against her, pushing his will towards her, picturing his strength pouring into her.

He didn't mean to sleep, he didn't want to risk losing even a minute with her but he had nothing left to give, his body needed to recharge. His eyes fluttered closed, he prayed it would be a dreamless sleep.

Chapter Twenty-Eight

Sunday morning came and with it no solution to cure Sarah.

"I think it's time we bring Alex in," Adam whipped his head towards Penny, anger coursed through him at what her statement implied. She held her hands up defensively, "You said your peace yesterday, he should get a turn too."

Adam was forced to swallow the bile that had risen in his throat, he didn't know if he was strong enough to be here when Alex said his goodbye. Finally, he nodded, "Okay, call Asald."

Everyone stood frozen, even though Penny had suggested he knew she didn't want to actually do it. Sebastian stood from the chair he had slept in, "I'll get Alex." He paused, he likely hoped someone would offer to take the errand from him. "I'll be back." His shoulders slumped as he turned to leave.

"WE GOT IT!" Yelling down the hall had everyone jumping. Dr. Larson ran in so fast he slammed against the door trying to stop himself. "We figured it out," Adam stepped back to let Seren and Alizon get closer. "She was poisoned with Strychnine, Seren actually figured it out and Alizon had the plant we need for treatment."

The room stood in shock as the three practitioners injected multiple substances into Sarah.

"She's going to be okay, without meaning to we did the best thing possible by intubating her early. With some activated charcoal and the curare extract, she'll wake up soon." Dr. Larson was smiling from ear to ear.

"Well, wake up isn't the right word exactly, they are usually mentally alert even though their body is shutting down. Stay close by and she'll be talking to you soon enough." Alizon squeezed Adam's hand, "Now if you will excuse me, I haven't slept in twenty-eight hours and I'd like to go find my bed."

"That sounds like a good plan to me, I'm going to go crash until tomorrow." Seren paused by the door, turning towards Sebastian, "this was definitely intentional, I'll fill you in after I get some sleep."

Chapter Twenty-Nine

It took a couple of hours but slowly Sarah's color returned, her breathing improved enough they were able to take out the tube. The wait for her to open her eyes was torture, no one could be sure she wouldn't have any side effects from the poisoning.

"How dare you try to kill yourself," the hoarse whisper from Sarah's lips sounded angelic to Adam even if she was trying to admonish him. "You couldn't die because you were meant for me, you were just born a few centuries too soon."

Adam laughed through the tears, "You come back from the brink of death and you bring jokes?" He leaned forward and kissed her, he didn't care that her lips were dry and cracked, he wanted nothing more than to crawl into the bed and hold her forever. He thought he had been doomed to an eternity of solitude, now he knew he was just waiting for the right person to come along.

Not only had she revived his will to live but she also succeeded in reviving his ability to love.

Dear Reader,

I hope you enjoyed this introduction to Black Hollow. Sheri Lyn and I have many tales to tell of this quirky town and we've invited a few guest authors to write in it as well. To keep up with town happenings visit www.blackhollowtown.com

Adam, Sarah and the gang will be back in future stories.

While you wait consider checking out one of my other books at www.cassidykoconnor.com

To learn more about Sheri Lyn's other titles please visit www.sherilynauthor.com

The blood was rushing in his veins and he could feel his heartbeat in his throat. Something was following him, it was above him, behind him, it was everywhere and he couldn't get away. With the next turn, he skidded to a stop realizing it was a dead end, the creature had trapped him.

"Who are you, what do you want?"

"Are you scared?"

The whisper was so close he spun around, but no one was there. The only light bulb in the area burst to his left, making him spin again. The shadows grew longer, increasing his terror.

"Come out and face me like a man!" The quiver in his voice belied his confidence.

"You're no man, you are a coward."

This time the voice came from the other end of the alley. Spotting some pipes laying against the wall, he slunk toward them and bent to pick one up. Before he could right himself, the pipe was knocked away and a steel grip closed around his throat, pushing him up against the wall.

"Wh...what are you?" His eyes were bulging, trying to take in the sight that must be wrong.

"I want you to feel the same fear your family does. I want you to feel the pain you have inflicted on them ten times over."

With a punch to the gut, he bent over only to be kneed in the face. The beating continued till he was wobbling on his knees, barely conscious.

With giant wings, the creature lifted off the ground slightly, raising his fist one last time as he stared the man down. "You will never harm another person as long as you live or it will be the last thing you do."

The fist to his jaw caused a crunching noise to reverberate down the alley. The creature flew away, leaving the man unconscious in a puddle of his own blood and urine.

One

"Penelope, another case just came in. Maria is asking for your help."

I can't help sighing as I hang my head wearily.

"Thanks, Consuela, I'll be right down."

As I look around my sanctuary, I'm reluctant to leave and face the crisis waiting for me downstairs. A woman can only listen to so many stories of sadness and violence before fearing for her own sanity. I have worked for the St. Anne's Women's Shelter for a little over a year now and while I often cry with the women and children who come in, I never doubt I'm doing exactly what I should be. I just wish there weren't so many people in need to begin with. When it gets to be too much, I escape to the roof for a quick break. No one else comes up, they believe the statues around the roof are demons. In reality, it's a really old building with cool gargoyle statues spaced all around the perimeter. There is a really large one at the center that I'm particularly fond of and often lay across. I named him Frank because he's big and tough looking and reminds me of my dad.

"Well, Frank, I should have known the full moon would bring in more cases. I'll be back later." Climbing off the statue, I stretch and feel an ache in my lower back. "Man, I need to start bringing up a blanket, you aren't very comfortable to lay on."

I shake my head as I head inside. If anyone knew I named the statues and talked to them they would probably have me locked away.

With a tug, I pull the heavy door closed and lock it up. Consuela is waiting a few steps down from me with a twinkle in her eye.

"So how was your date the other night with the school teacher?"

"I thought it went really well up until he didn't answer my calls just like the rest of them. I am starting to think there is some kind of curse on me. How can I possibly have twelve bad first dates?"

"You aren't giving away the goods too soon, are you?"

"If you are asking if I am sleeping with them and they are hitting it and quitting, the answer is no. There wasn't more than a good night kiss and even that was only with a couple of them."

"I'll say an extra prayer for you at church on Sunday and who knows, maybe thirteen will be your lucky number!"

I chuckle at her enthusiasm, I knew dating would be harder when I moved to the city. I didn't think I would be a complete failure at it though. Maybe I'm destined to be alone and give everything I have serving others. Maybe I should consider becoming a nun? Let's face it, I like sex and not just in a casual once in a while kind of way. My libido is really high and my toys just aren't keeping me satisfied. I need to find a man soon or I may combust.

I shake my head to clear my thoughts and prepare myself for our new guests. If I'm not completely in control of my emotions, these intakes can be much more upsetting for me. "Okay, let's do this."

I follow Consuela out of the stairwell and to the conference room we use to interview new families. Only the slightest hitch in my step belies my shock at seeing the bruises and bandages covering the woman's face. Even though she is in her twenties or thirties, her face shows the tough life she has lived. Her son is cuddled against her side. He looks to be about six or seven years old, but his eyes that peek at me show a child who has already lost the innocence of youth. Thankfully he looks physically okay. I don't think it will ever get easier to see a battered woman or child.

"Penelope, this is Sarah and her son, Alex. We've just finished the paperwork, can you take them to room 304 and get them some food on the way up?"

Kneeling down in front of Alex, I give him my best smile. "Hi, Alex, my name is Penny. Are you hungry?"

Only the slightest nod tells me he heard. Sarah smiles shyly and stands up with Alex glued to her side.

"Follow me and I'll show you around."

We take a short walk down the hall, I stop and show them the artwork hung down both sides. A lot of the kids here are very talented and deserve to show their creations for everyone to see, even if they don't have their own fridges to hang them on. We enter a large room organized into smaller rooms, my apartment could probably fit in here at least four times over. One corner has tables for meals, another corner has a library and computers, the third corner has shelves of games and toys, and the fourth corner has couches and a large T.V. It's after nine p.m. so there are only a few women and children in each area.

"This is the common area where the families can come together to hang out. You can come down anytime and fix yourselves a snack. Everyone chips in around here and takes turns cooking meals and cleaning the common areas."

I slide a glass of milk over to Alex and hand Sara a bottle of water. "Turkey or ham sandwiches?"

Sarah's timid voice cracks as she says they will both have turkey.

"Good choice, that's my favorite, too. Breakfast is at eight thirty, lunch is at twelve and dinner is served at six thirty."

I slide the sandwiches over and sit across from them in silence. Sometimes silence is more comforting than anything else.

"How long can we stay here?"

"You can stay as long as you need and we have counselors you can schedule time with. We also have a couple of lawyers who donate their time to answer legal questions. We will be here for you as long as you need us. When you are ready to go out on your own, we'll help you find jobs, apartments and anything else you need. I promise you are safe here."

We lapse into silence again and let them finish their food, it doesn't take long and they both anxiously jump up to clean their dishes.

"Okay, let's go see your rooms."

The building is old and the elevator tiny; we squeeze in and Alex eagerly pushes the three button when I tell him to.

A quick tour of their living room and bedroom then I leave them to rest. I don't know what they've been through tonight, but I know sleep is the best thing for them now. Who knows the last time they felt safe closing their eyes.

My watch beeps quietly, my shift is finally over, one more thing before I can go home...

"I'm telling you, Frank, you should have seen them. They were pale, scared and exhausted," my back cracks as I stretch in my favorite gargoyle's arms. "These night shifts are killer, I can't wait for the sunrise then I can head home and crash for the entire day."

I lay peacefully watching the sky slowly change color, the city waking up. I love sunrises, they give me hope that today is a new day and something magical could happen. The sun crests over the buildings, shining brightly till I have to look away.

"All right, that's it for me. I'll see you tomorrow, big guy."

Two

"So Alex, you have been here two weeks and I still never see you playing with any other kids. Don't you think it's time to make a friend?"

His shoulder barely moves as he shrugs, I see him looking out the window of the conference room at the kids playing with legos.

"Come on, we'll go together."

Jumping up, I hold out my hand and release a breath of relief when his tiny hand grabs mine. Every kid here has been through similar situations so I have no doubt they will welcome him easily.

"Hey guys, this is Alex. We were wondering if we can join you?"

Marissa, a beautiful girl who has been with us for three months, jumps up with legos in hand.

"I'm building a castle, want to help?"

Every kid stops playing and stares at the block she's holding out, no one knowing what he will do. I can't help the tears stinging my eyes when his tiny fingers wrap around the block and he follows her to the table.

An hour later, we've built the largest castle in the city and my back is killing me.

"Okay, guys, I'm done for the day. I'll see you tomorrow."

"Are you going to see the bird man before you go?"

"What do you mean, Alex?"

"You're going up to the roof to hang out with the bird man, right?"

"Oh, the gargoyle statues? Yeah, I like to sit up there."

"They aren't statues, I've seen them flying around."

Um, okay, he's just starting to open up so I don't want to argue. I am a little concerned, he's losing touch with reality to escape his problems.

"I'm jealous, they've never flown for me. I guess you must be something special."

With a smile, he turns and goes back to playing.

I grab my purse out of my locker and head up to the roof. The bird men are right where I left them, it would be pretty cool to see them fly though.

"Frank, I'm upset with you, Alex says you can fly. I'm hurt you showed him and not me, I thought we were friends?"

The stone gargoyle stares ahead like I'm not even there; maybe I'm the one losing touch with reality. I curl against him and wait for the sun to set, nature sure knows how to paint a masterpiece.

"Well, that's it for me, I have a hot date tonight and if I don't get some action, I may just lose my mind. I need to get laid badly! Keep everyone safe while I'm gone."

******

With a knife to his throat, the poor old man whimpers in terror. He's walked these same streets every day for forty years and never had a bit of trouble.

"Give me your wallet and your watch and I'll let you walk out of here."

With shaking hands, the old man passes them over, praying he will take them and leave. He should have known better, with a hard punch to the stomach the old man doubles over in pain.

As the thief pulls his arm back to punch again, he hears a swooshing noise and spins around. The creature flying toward him can't be real, terror like he has never experienced shows in his own eyes. The vice grip around his throat sends him flying against the opposite wall.

"You think it's okay to harm people that are weaker than you? It's your turn to experience their pain."

With a few punches, the thief is unconscious on the ground. The old man still cowers against the opposite wall, watching as the creature takes out the thief's wallet and empties it before turning, tossing his wallet and watch back to him and taking off into the sky.

The old man can't hold back the moan as he pushes himself up and takes off, leaving the alley behind him. He has no desire to be there when the thief wakes up. His brain unwilling to accept what his eyes saw, he chooses to say a prayer for his savior and forget it ever happened.

ABOUT THE AUTHOR

Cassidy lives in the Tampa, Florida area with her high school sweetheart, their three children, one crazy senior dog, a guinea pig, a skinny pig and the newest love of her life her puppy Flynn. She loves reading and going to the movies but not nearly as much as she enjoys watching her kids either playing ball or performing with one of their instruments. She also loves travelling and hopes to one day watch a baseball game in every MLB stadium in the country.

To learn more about Cassidy please visit her online at

www.cassidykoconnor.com.

You can also find her on Facebook at

www.facebook.com/cassidykoconnorauth

or

She always welcomes new friends and encourages readers to reach out to her.

Other Books by the Author

Sassy Ever After

In My Mate's Sight

In My Mate's Defense

Paranormal Dating Agency

My Oath To You

Stand Alones

Broken Dreams

Forever Yours, Casey

The Laird's Promise

Loving the Monster Within

To Steal a Prince's Heart

Wicked Wonderland Retreat

The Love's Protector Series

Awakening Her Desires

The Evolution of Sam

Finding His Swing